MARY BENSON

was born in Pretoria in 1919. Her father, who had emigrated from Dublin in 1899, was a hospital adminstrator; her mother's family, who were among the 1920 Settlers from London, were prominent in "Native" administration. During her childhood the family lived next door to the prison where several of her friends would later be incarcerated. After matriculating Mary Benson travelled to Europe and America — her first published article was about a visit to Hollywood in 1939. Joining the South African Women's Army, she became Personal Assistant to various British Generals in the Middle East, Italy, Greece and Vienna. Subsequently, in 1946, she worked for UNRRA in Germany.

During three years as secretary to David Lean, she read *Cry, the Beloved Country*. Its profound effect led to her work with the Reverend Michael Scott in Britain and at the United Nations, campaigning against apartheid, until, in 1957, she became secretary of the Treason Trials Defence Fund in Johannesburg. Ill health forced her resignation and she turned to writing: her biography of Tshekedi Khama was published in 1960; *The African Patriots*, a history of the African National Congress followed in 1963.

Mary Benson then became the first South African to testify at the United Nations. A year later, in 1964, she returned to South Africa and, while reporting on obscure political trials for the *Observer*, gathered unique material about the hitherto neglected Eastern Cape. This experience inspired her later novel, *At the Still Point* (1969). Early in 1966 she was banned and placed under house arrest in Johannesburg. Since leaving the country, she has been prohibited from returning. Her other publications include an updated history of the ANC, *South Africa, the Struggle for a Birthright* (1966, republished as a classic in 1986) and a life of *Nelson Mandela* (1986). In 1983 she edited Athol Fugard's *Notebooks*. Articles on South African politics and theatre have appeared in British and American newspapers and her plays for BBC radio include an adaptation of *At the Still Point*. Recently she has been working with Harry Belafonte on a mini-series about South Africa for American television.

She lives in London.

VIRAGO
MODERN
CLASSIC

NUMBER
280

MARY BENSON

AT THE
STILL POINT

WITH A NEW AFTERWORD BY
THE AUTHOR

/ / / / / / / / / / / / / / /

"... *at the still point,*
there the dance is ..."
—T. S. Eliot

Virago

To A.F., A.P., and A.F., through whom I learned to know and to love my country.

Also to A.K. and P.R., but especially the latter, for excellent and most generous criticism and encouragement.

Lines from "Burnt Norton" in *The Four Quartets*, by T.S. Eliot, reprinted by permission of Faber and Faber Ltd.
Lines from *The Rebel* and *Resistance, Rebellion and Death* by A. Camus, Penguin Books.
Lines from an Ingrid Jonker poem in *Classic Magazine*, translated by Athol Fugard, Johannesburg, South Africa.
Lines from *Auschwitz: A Doctor's Eye-Witness Account* by Dr. Miklos Nyiszli, Panther Books. Foreword by Bruno Bettelheim.

Published by VIRAGO PRESS Limited 1988
41 William IV Street, London WC2N 4DB

First published in the USA by Gambit, Boston 1969
First published in Great Britain by Chatto & Windus 1971

British Library Cataloguing in Publication Data
Benson, Mary
At the still point. —— (Virago modern classics).
I. Title
823 [F]   PR9369.3.B/

ISBN 0-86068-937-9

Printed in Great Britain by Cox and Wyman of Reading, Berks

South Africa's sabotage trials of 1963-64 were over, but from 1965 onward hundreds of Africans were brought to trial in remote villages. And early in 1965, a distinguished white lawyer, on trial as a Communist, disappeared and went underground. These facts of South African history provide the framework for this novel with its wholly fictional characters.

GLOSSARY

ASSEGAAI.	*Zulu spear.*
BERG.	*Mountain.*
BIOSCOPE.	*Cinema.*
BRAAI.	*Abbreviation for braaivleis—barbecue (Afrikaans).*
DOEK.	*Scarf worn about the head (Afrikaans).*
DOMINEE.	*Dutch Reformed Church minister (Afrikaans).*
DORP.	*Village (Afrikaans).*
IMPIMPI.	*Traitor, informer (Xhosa).*
KOPJE.	*Hill (Afrikaans).*
KWELA.	*African township dance.*
PANGA.	*Long, sharp-bladed instrument.*
RONDAVEL.	*Round room with a thatched roof.*
SHEBEEN.	*Illegal drinking place in African townships.*
TSOTSIS.	*Young toughs or delinquents from African townships.*

Part One

Chapter 1

T HE PLANE LURCHED UNDER MY STOCKINGED FEET. MY
eyes opened to daylight, but muted. We were flying
through clouds. I had slept heavily, exhausted by uncertainty. I pressed my face to the window and looked down.
A break in the clouds, and there far below were the patched
and speckled expanses of Africa.

Perplexity surged again. And alarm: I'm crazy, what the
hell am I doing here?

The thought of Roger grew more insistent—"You're a
scream, Anne baby, I just love you"—the exact inflection
with his drawl exaggerated in the way he had of deliberately rendering endearments ambivalent. My mind shook
off the memory, only to be assailed by another, of our tired
argument, that last night in New York. "I am not walking
out," I'd said. Calmly, reasonably, I had explained: "It is
simply a question of maintaining independence." And he:
"Don't fool yourself, baby! The fact is you're running
away."

Nonsense. Why, when I was a child and turned up at
Grandpa's house, suddenly, "Quite right," he'd say, "as-

sert your independence!" his old eyes gleaming commendation . . . Roger's eyes, the densely curling lashes, that sideways grin. Our first date, at Sardi's, the small table, the eyeball-to-eyeball encounter. Such wit! How we laughed. Then we turned serious, and I asserted: "If one can only give oneself straight, honestly, one must surely reach, understand, the other . . ."

Again I pressed my face to the window and felt its surface, cool. "A kind of ironic cool." That's what drew Roger—at first—then: "Honesty, doll? Well, I'll be honest. You're all the time on the outside. Outside!"

Breakfast was being served, and while my feet searched until they found my shoes, I resolved simply to be a traveler. My fork cut into the omelette. My bare arm was jostled by my neighbour's which, heavy, hairy, in a short-sleeved shirt, overlapped my seat. Obliquely I looked at his face, unshaved with jutting underlip.

"Finest way to travel," Grandpa once said, "is to sit right here in my study in Johannesburg"—his hand was caressing books on the Nile, the Amazon, the Mississippi—"no flies, no beggars, no tourists." Grandpa's study, cool dim still, as his grizzled head bent over Marius, or the *Odyssey* . . . Outside, the movement of birds and insects in the afternoon heat. And I on the footstool beside him, my knees nudging my cheekbones as I hunched there while his voice dwelt on some passage . . . perhaps from *Moby Dick*, Queequeg and Ishmael, the two of them cozy in a double bed, legs entwined, the unhurried intimate conversation you can only have in bed . . .

The plane jolted, then swayed. I'd forgotten the fury of

these brief African storms. I flinched and welcomed fright, which was more positive than uncertainty, than apathy . . . Father came into his own in a bad storm, his thin upright form silhouetted as he stood at the window watching the lightning, oblivious of Mom and Lance and me and our concerted agitation: "Come away from the window, Dad, for goodness' sake, do you want to be struck dead?"

In Nairobi from the cage of the terminal I watched the storm's retreat. On the sofa opposite me sprawled several Italians, hand luggage labelled DAR ES SALAAM. The nymphomanic-looking little girl in high-heeled boots, her hair streaming black from under a white sun helmet, pawed an epicene man in a beige frock coat . . . I must remember to tell Roger.

I heard our flight number called.

Outside, my skin responded to the warm glow, far now from the chill of New York's December. The sun blazed suddenly from a gigantic sky. Beyond the runways the grass grew tall, the trees crouched close to the rain-drenched earth . . . The jet's roar swelled to screaming.

The plane flew steadily south. The land below lay limit-less under the haze of sunlight. Funny, so many people escaping from South Africa and here I was escaping into it. Yet with some sense of reality, now. Gone are the days . . . Mom swathed to the ankles in lace or chiffon, from finger-tips to elbows in white kid gloves, and Dad in what Lance and I called his military mood, setting off for Government House . . . The meringue they had noticed under a rose tree with false teeth embedded! Dad hid snacks in a hand-kerchief to bring to us—"With the compliments of His Excellency the Governor-General," he said . . . The good old days when Smuts was Prime Minister. Then, in 1948, disaster! The victory of those "accursed Boers," as Dad called them. Still in power now. Not even the sabotage moved them . . . and now the sabotage is over. Sounds like a song. No Bob Dylan there . . . Grandpa disapproved heartily of our student protests, so anaemic they'd seem to-day . . . he said Proust warned you'd have no time to think of Literature if you ran round pursuing the Triumph of Justice . . . Since childhood he had filled me with other dreams of other places and other times; then, in the clouds that massed at sunset, we'd discover Olympus, Valhalla . . . But what would I have done without him? When Father emerged from his workshop, as he liked to call it, expres-sionless, eyes opaque, breath revealing, and Mom in retalia-tion headed for her bridge club, a horde of women intent over their clutched cards in a smoke-filled room, while outside the bright sun dazed, then I would race to Grand-pa's . . . with words he soothed my cramping pain: "You wait, Apple, when you're of age your legacy will come, then you will travel." "Apple of Grandpa's eye!" Lance chanted. "Green-eyed Annie Apple! Remember what hap-pened to the apple on that chap's head!" . . . But it was I shot him with an arrow—thank God it missed his eye. Guilt pings through me even now! He deserved it, rotten tease he was, and fair game I was too! The time he dared me to put a millipede in my mouth; I was petrified . . . vile taste! Ugh. He said my tongue would drop out—I kept rushing to the mirror and ever so carefully pulling it . . . Lance, vastly improved. Life? Canada? Or his wife. Mom too . . .

6

Funny how, at the same moment, we all agreed we were much nicer now . . . Pity Father hadn't lived to enjoy it.

Morning coffee. My neighbour ordered brandy and ginger ale . . . I remembered Roger's double bourbon the moment he boarded a plane, the only way to rout the panic that haunted him . . . Why in a superjet should the coffee taste of plastic? Why have I lost all comic sense . . . irony fled . . . and I fleeing. My hands reached for the earphones of Inflight Music, settled them to my ears, and turned on to jazz—piano meditates, bass echoes, extends a phrase . . . filling my skin with music . . . now, trumpets and saxophone convolute through the bones of my skull . . .

Below I could see the faded green veld of the Transvaal. I clambered over my neighbour and went to the toilet, where, faced by my winter-pale reflection, I considered the eyes—definitely anxious—and the mouth—too large . . . at least the straight fair hair was shining. All the same I brushed until my elbow sagged, then brushed my teeth, splashed my face with cold water and—as I completed my makeup with pale lipstick, eyeliner and scent—I felt mettle return to my spirit. With a lighter step I walked back to my seat.

"Fasten your seat belts, please!" Hell, I'd meant to use the journey to get things clarified; instead, just a lot of noise in my mind, hours and hours wasted, never to be retrieved. Newness of life—lovely idea, each moment a potential fresh start—if only you weren't stuck with all the preceding moments . . .

Johannesburg appeared below. Gardens with turquoise

glinting pools. The yellow minedumps were unchanged. Skyscrapers. New highways. A junior New York.

We were landing at Jan Smuts airport . . . and came down the steps into hot sunshine. I breathed the rarefied high-veld air, glanced at the clear blue sky, and started off across the tarmac toward people waving. Shula and Ben— how alike they suddenly looked! Cousin Patrick with Sally —had he sacrificed his Sunday golf then? And, next to Shula, Jake, pointing at me, showing me to his small sisters. I stopped in my tracks and pointed at him . . . they were all laughing.

The terminal had changed in two years, there was no longer the claustrophobic cubicle, the intimidating interview . . . now, instead, in the arrivals hall a smiling official welcomed each one of us: "Have a good time!" And why not . . .

Chapter 2

"F ANCY GOING TO A BUNCH OF INTELLECTUALS FOR NEW
Year's," said Patrick, and chuckled. "But have a good
time, dear."

I promised to try. I also could be ironic, and regarded his
neck, thinking how . . . intact, that was the word, he
looked in his dinner jacket. Was his collar tight? All the
same the black and white formality flattered his rosy-
tanned, handsome face. "You too," I added.

"But of course," he said, giving a pat to his cummerbund.
"You can rely on the Country Club to do you proud."
Handing me the keys for one of his cars, he accompanied
me from the drawing room.

The keys struck cold into the palm of my hand. Had it
been a terrible mistake, to come back? In the hall I said
thanks, and good night. From beyond Patrick's shoulder
my mirrored face smiled brightly.

Sally was coming downstairs, blond and happy in smoky-
blue chiffon, looking like one of the angels on her Christ-
mas cards. "Have a gorgeous time," she said, and, as she
kissed me lightly, "Try and forget whatever it is that's
bothering you."

I was touched. Her perspicacity in intimate matters often took me by surprise.

"Mind you take care," she insisted. "It's a bad night . . . so many drunken drivers."

"Yes, do take care," said Patrick. "Crime's on the up and up. Remember, always drive with the car doors locked and the windows up. Tsotsis are two a penny these days."

At the Lowens' house the front door stood open . . . Ben came toward me, not much taller than I, cozy, bespectacled, his eyes narrowed in laughter. "Anne love, you look smashing, the sun suits you."

And Shulamuth appeared, hardly changed since school, still favouring handwoven linens. She drew me inside, toward a blur of people, welcoming: "Anne! You here! How nice!"

"How *is* London?" someone asked, and another, "but I thought you were in New York?"

I said quickly, "I live in London, but was visiting my mother in Vancouver; I stopped by in New York." Stopped by . . . it was one way of describing the time with Roger.

"What a way to put it," said Ben.

I stared. How could he know ?

"Haven't you heard?" He turned to the others. "Anne's become a journalist of repute, you should see her work . . ." Relief had me laughing before I could mock his exaggerations.

A girl, deep-tanned in a brief white dress, said it sounded intriguing and could she interview me, not social column stuff, she said, and Ben introduced her. "Helen Mills, one of our best political reporters."

"But sweetie," interrupted a woman in violet, "how can you bear to come back to this place?"

I heard myself say, "Oh, I don't know, there's always the sun." How corny can you get, I wondered, but rattled on. "Besides, England's . . . it's lost interest, the middle class complain that nothing is real . . ." I broke off before my overvivacious voice could compound the clichés.

Ben, his arm about my shoulders, grinned. "Shit hey, if they want reality this is the place to come!" Dear Ben, he liked to say it was being so cheerful kept him fit when every other liberal had ulcers or asthma or a chronic sense of doom. I greatly wanted not to talk, simply to drift, perhaps absorb, but I was affected by their welcome and sensed, in the questions fired at me about people and plays and politics, a desperate isolation, a hunger for the free air and ideas outside.

"What will you do?" someone asked, "now that you've come home?"

" Jacob!" Chubby, in pyjamas, he appeared with an air half purposeful, half appealing, clearly Ben's son. Shulamuth, flushed, tendrils of hair clinging to her high forehead, scolded, "It's nearly quarter to ten! Go back to bed!" and after a verbal scuffle managed to bribe him with a bowl of potato crisps.

Have I "come home," I wondered. If I could feel "at home" anywhere it might be with Ben and Shula, and through the chatter I willed myself firmly *here*, in this familiar room. Deliberately I studied the Persian carpet, a striped linen cushion . . . Politeness, that's my trouble. Roger had been goaded to the point of shouting, "Screw you! You're just too cool to live, baby!" So *here* I am, but in a vacuum and as long as it's not filled—no use, there was no going back . . . I renewed concentration on what was in front of my eyes. Out of the blur and into focus came a dress, pink and orange, large-patterned, mine, beside it another, violet, worn by the woman I didn't know, with black shoes and pale stockings. She was talking to Ben, his face creamy-beige and swarthy-chinned above the buttoned collar of his Italian shirt. The woman's face loomed larger, she was laughing—what cold eyes—her laugh came loud, I was laughing and agreeing but I hadn't heard a word. Dimly there was music, the staircase in the distance, the tail of Shula's cat disappearing up it, layers of images and sounds and, just beyond the violet dress, shelves crammed with books. I peered at the print down the spine of one . . . Roger, gazing at a Marino Marini sculpture in the Museum of Modern Art, taking my hand in his . . . yet he could be bloody rude, and yet again . . . the night he'd just put out the light and something I said made him laugh like mad. He'd turned over then toward me and kissed me. Not the usual engulfing, but sweetly and precisely. "You're a scream, Anne baby. I just love you." The only time either of us ever talked of love . . . there was that much honesty between us . . .

Ben hurried to welcome a new arrival, a big man, bald, with glasses—Keith Gibbon, on a visit from Oxford. He'd been lionized at Cousin Patrick's the night before . . . an "intellectual," yes, but cultivated in the hothouse of All Souls, that was something else again, exotic, by no means one of a "bunch." He was clearly more at home here than with my cousins. I smiled warmly at him.

"Ah, the prodigal," he greeted me and shook hands—a soft, diffident, British handshake—before turning to Ben, who complimented him on a lecture he had given and urged him to explain the Platonic reference again for those who had missed it. "But sit down, Professor, let me give you a drink. Scotch? Soda?"

Don't be an idiot, I told myself, going on about Roger, like a driver stuck in bottom gear, grinding along . . .

". . . Plato's allegory of the Cave," Keith Gibbon was saying. "I find it extraordinarily telling for this country." Oh no, I thought, British diplomacy, why bother . . . But clever of him to choose those heavy-rimmed spectacles, a nice aberrant touch for a scholarly type. What a pity, those long strands arranged across his crown, I'll bet the wind perpetually disarranges . . .

"Do go on, Professor," said Shulamuth. Lovely word, perpetually . . . I rolled it about in my mind as if it were a pebble.

"Well, in the Cave men were chained in darkness, only able to see shadows, hence believing in their reality." He had a pleasing manner, didactic yet lively. "But I see chains of bigotry, human beings living with illusions." I'd misjudged, this was intriguing. "If one of them moved toward the light, became strong and independent enough to face the truth, he would feel happy to have changed. But should he return, and try to tell his former companions what he had discovered, how illusory their shadows were, they would chastise him, they might even become violent . . . As a matter of fact, Mr. Lowen," he smiled engagingly at Ben, "your excellent article last Sunday provoked this concept." Ben looked gratified.

Illusions, where did they end and hypocrisy begin? . . . Roger. Startlingly, your hand on me. Your voice, that first time, "Look, we both want each other. We're both adult." Yes, I had wanted you. Past-perfect tense. But here, now, I feel contempt to think I pretended reluctance, that first time. Hypocrisy! Yes, and again now, for without you life has been wide open, vacant. Painful together, but painful apart . . .

Shulamuth addressed Gibbon: "Have you noticed, Professor, how fortunate we liberals are, hm? All the comfort of white supremacy, right? Without the guilty conscience of having voted for it."

Why Shula, I thought, that's a pretty witty observation. But you are a humbug . . . you're always plagued by guilt.

A girl was asking Gibbon for his first impressions.

Impressions . . . mine jostle till I feel like a bone being shaken by a dog. Bleached blue sky—such air, dry thin rare —cosmos thick along the roadside—miles of factories, British trade signs everywhere—scent of eucalyptus—Sally's remark, "You'll be surprised how sophisticated life is"; then, with her hand on the horn for some brown motorist swerving in front of us, "These Indians! Getting above themselves since one of them won the golf." The thrusting city with everything high, altitude buildings atmosphere— Shula's light reminder, "Of course, one never says anything on the telephone, and certain offices are bugged, and homes and cars"—the signs in butchers' windows: fillet 45 cents pets' meat boys' meat 15 cents—Patrick's confident, "A great boom! Never seen the market so strong!" —law and order and ninety days and what makes traitors —"Just time for a swim before our martinis or would you prefer vodka tonic?"—bougainvillea golden shower plumbago communists liberalists sickly humanists—and blacks, servants messengers truck drivers labourers policemen beggars, more blacks than ever before—and whites, suntanned with manifestly unreflective stares . . . Once I wouldn't have noticed . . .

Ben, refilling my glass and giving himself his usual ginger ale, asked after old friends in exile.

"I've never met one that wasn't homesick," I said. "The politicals I hardly see, but remember Peter Tembu? Who never lifted a finger at home? He's become a popular black nationalist on the New York to California circuit."

Ben was enchanted.

"Changed his name from Peter to Mbekeni," I went on. "At least in some places it pays to be black." And Fatso, I had heard he'd been impressive at a literary conference in Moscow.

"But he was a rabid anti-communist here," someone objected.

"Ah, well," said Ben, "given the right audience, anyone becomes political."

The odd thing about the party was that previously there would have been a dozen Africans present, some for real and some for show . . . now there were none . . . the

Lowens' black friends were all in exile or in jail . . . half
their white friends too.

A burst of laughter . . . Roger. More painful apart.
Perhaps . . . No! It's over. But what if I'm incapable of
loving? If it's as simple as that?

Impatiently I looked around for Shulamuth, searched
and found her in the kitchen. "I'm bored with myself," I
said, and laughed.

She looked at me and said sarcastically, "Lucky you, that
you can afford to be bored with yourself." Her unusually
biting tone jolted me. I beamed at her to placate.

"Cookie," she said, "I still, after all these years, can't
tell when you're being serious."

"Well, think of something I can do."

She had already forgiven me. "For a start, you can bring
these." She pushed two dishes toward me. "To the terrace."

Outside, the glow from the house dulled the stars but revealed a bed of nasturtiums, yellow and orange. The night
was fresh after the day's stifling heat. Between waves of
noise from neighbouring parties you could hear crickets.
The scent of petunia and tobacco plant was in the air. An
occasional moth fluttered.

The tanned girl in white, Helen Mills, was telling Ben,
"Seems things are hotting up, the S.B.—de Villiers and
Grobelaar actually—dropped in on me this morning,"
dropping the remark between pauses to light a cigarette.

Shulamuth explained to Gibbon: "Helen's talking about
the Special Branch. De Villiers is one of the most hated.
He's subtle, and fancies his power over women. Not with-

out reason." Then, in an aside to me, she added, "Curious, it seems danger stimulates people; sexually, I mean . . ."

"Grobelaar reminds me of a jumped-up hearse driver," said Helen.

A tall man said, "Dan Makhana once remarked that Grobelaar looks very horrible but he's not a bad fellow."

"How could he say that when Grobelaar helped send him to Robben Island!" protested Shula.

"A lot of crop-necked swine!"

"Sabotage! Bloody fool amateur messing about!" The voice spluttered from a man who looked docile, small, and neat. "Those idiots on trial today. It was all in their pockets when the police arrested them—notes on the techniques of war! Even a photo taken in Addis, like a blinking football team!"

Shulamuth blushed with indignation. "Colin, it's all very well, but you, you as an officer in the war, you got all the technical knowhow you needed, if you'd only offered some to those people, *then* you'd be entitled . . ."

No wonder we have a reputation for talking nothing but politics, I thought. But of course . . . this is not politics, this is life.

"It's a beautiful summer," said someone. Yes, it is. Beautiful. And it's a beautiful night and I'm glad I came back.

I could hear two journalist friends of Ben's debating the Springboks' prospects in the Cricket Test. I looked about for Keith Gibbon. He was with others, discussing the meadows of Oxford, *Zuleika Dobson;* I listened with idle detachment. His glance met mine and developed into a smile of concord.

Ben stood beside us, wanting us to meet someone. Gibbon excused himself and readily he and I went along with Ben, who rounded up a young man: Andrew Fox, a university lecturer, hefty, big-boned. I remembered him, a keen sportsman, good at rugby and tennis. The four of us settled in chairs, blue and white plastic-cushioned. "Our new garden suite," explained Ben, "a present from Shulamuth's old man." Something about Andrew Fox was puzzling me. Before, there'd been a positive quality—beyond his physical strength—a brightness. Now, it was as if he had been drained.

Ben was leaning forward to look earnestly into Gibbon's face. "Andrew was held under the ninety days' law. In solitary confinement, with prolonged interrogation. The Statue Torture."

Andrew's expression did not change. Gibbon, who had listened gravely, said, "I heard they'd picked that up from the French in Algeria."

"Yes. The nice guys soft-soap after the sadists break you." Andrew sounded uninterested. Then, perhaps responding to Gibbon's patent concern or perhaps out of his own seeming unconcern, he went on. "They force you to stand in one spot, hour after hour, you lose all count . . . until your resistance packs up . . . after one particularly long dose of this Statue treatment, I was dropping when the chummy crew came on duty. They begged me to keep up, for their sakes, and I did." His voice stopped. From inertia, one would say.

Ben spoke up. "I remember your telling me, Andy, that you held on for about another fifteen hours before you collapsed." And Ben turned to Gibbon once more: "Then the bastards clap Andy on the back. Congratulate him! 'Shit man, you've done a good job. Hang but we're proud of you. We think you've broke the blerry record!' "

Several people had gathered to listen. They must know it by heart.

Andrew, who seemed not to mind Ben's interventions, took up the story: "So they sent for the lieutenant to check. I was so grateful to them. And the lieutenant arrives. He says, well he's not sure, and by this time I was howling, I felt on the edge of a precipice, I was praying I had broken the record. Then the lieutenant says, 'Yes. From my experience you have set up a record.' "

"Can you beat that for crazy inquisitors?" asked Ben, and laughed. And was silent. Suddenly the reality of it had him by the throat. He took off his spectacles and as he started to rub them with a handkerchief, shortsightedly he looked around.

At all costs I knew one must keep one's eyes from encountering other eyes, especially those of Andrew Fox, whose hands, I noticed, remained absolutely still on his knees as he sat there, breathing the night air.

It struck me, precisely, that the victim had spoken without a trace of expression, while Ben, the propagandist, had been animated. And it also struck me that the listeners attended partly because it was a fantastically outrageous story, partly because this was the least, the very least, you could do.

"That vicious bullyboy Grunauer," said Helen Mills, "invites his chums to watch an interrogation just when he's about to put the pressure on. His idea of entertainment. One of his friends at least had the grace to vomit."

"And it all goes on right next door to the American Embassy!" said Shulamuth. She shook her head, incredulously.

Keith Gibbon turned back to Andrew Fox.

"I've had enough," said Andrew. "It's hopeless here. There's nothing can be done. They've got us right there." And he made his first positive gesture, pressing a large blunt thumb into the palm of his hand and twisting it, this way and that, hard.

From a nearby group I picked up a fragment of conversation—". . . a bit farfetched to identify Genet with Herzog." "Ah, but both make the point that the good has been devalued . . ." I thought it promised comparative relief . . . better still, to go to the end of the terrace, where a few couples were dancing to music from a record player.

Keith Gibbon's voice kept me in my chair. In the thirties, he was saying, one of his friends at Oxford had been a German, a Rhodes scholar—I calculated, that made Gibbon what, forty-eight? Fifty? He didn't look it—who subsequently was in the plot against Hitler. "Those young men who gave their lives," he said quietly, "they were amateurs, too. The professionals were on the other side." He paused. "I think it's true that the German resistance failed because no political"—he emphasized the word—"no political power came to their aid, neither from within nor from outside."

How apt, how appallingly apt. As if time stood still under the southern sky. As if the dimension of our lives, our responsibilities, our fate, was suddenly revealed . . . For a moment I felt I was one of them. Deadly discomfited. And Gibbon went on, "There was absolutely no possibility of organizing a popular movement. Not of revolutionary force. Not under such a tyranny."

Ben spoke. "Did I tell you about my encounter with the customs chappie at the airport? No? A couple of months ago I flew in from Rhodesia . . . I had a paperback I was reading, a history of Africa. Well, this customs chap seized the book, took it to his supervisor. 'Cawnfuscate?' he asked. 'Yus, cawnfuscate,' his senior said." Ben's eyes crinkled in self-enjoyment. "So, last Thursday, when I came back from Salisbury"—now his face was serious— "what do I see as I come off the plane and start to cross the tarmac but a ruddy official watching me, dead-grim. I thought, shit man, they're waiting for me this time! Tell the truth, I was half flattered . . . and this chap comes up to me all confidential—actually by now I felt pretty scared!—and then he mutters to me, 'Your fly's undone.' "

There was a shout of laughter. Demurely Ben busied himself filling glasses. I drifted away across the lawn to the lower terrace where hibiscus and tamarisk screened off the glow from the house so that the stars for the first time acquired their full brilliance. Keith Gibbon's quietly stated analogy terrified yet excited me.

"Anne Dawson?" A tall, very dark man stood beside me. "Shulamuth told me to find you and introduce myself." His voice inspired tranquillity. I'd noticed him while Gibbon was telling us about the German resistance; he had listened and not spoken. He held out a hand, bony and firm, looked at me with frank consideration, and explained, "I'm

Alan Lemkovitz, an old friend of the Lowens."

Lemkovitz and Lowen, like a music-hall joke, descendants of refugees from Russia, the Baltic, from one pogrom or another, from abortive revolutions or poverty.

"All of you tonight," I confided; "somehow it's as if there's been a shipwreck . . ."

"Yes . . . yes, you could say we're the lucky few huddled together on a raft . . . not much sense of direction" —his smile was wry—"attempting to keep each other's spirits up with our small jokes . . . some of us with little in common but anger . . . and our feeling for those who've gone down."

"How you all stay so gallant!"

He shrugged. "It's a question of survival."

"Yes." And each morning, I thought, the sun streams through the window to wake you while from the eucalyptus trees behind the house doves croon and from the kitchen comes the chatter of servants preparing the early cup of tea. "What was the sabotage like?" I asked.

"Desperate. Foolhardy, tremendously brave. God knows if it was worth it in terms of men we need. Mandela, Makhana . . . now on Robben Island for life . . ." He gazed down. Beyond the rocky hillside of the garden we could see the lights of the northern suburbs, a great expanse glittering in the darkness below.

"What do you do?" I asked.

"I'm an advocate."

"What sort of work?"

"It used to be commercial, nowadays virtually all political."

After a while, "I never can find the Southern Cross," I said, "when I first get back."

He pointed to four evenly spaced stars, an insignificant constellation. The breeze must have dropped; we could no longer hear the other parties, only the crickets, unceasing.

"Can you hear the stars twinkling?" I asked.

He was hesitant.

"That's what I thought the sound of crickets was, when I was small."

He suddenly looked cheerful. "You must tell that to the twins . . ."

Clang! Dang! Ang! Ang! . . . ang . . . ang . . . an almighty clamorous din broke out of the darkness.

"Don't be alarmed," he said, laughing. "Have you forgotten? The servants everywhere, their traditional act, banging the telegraph poles."

Shouts, songs, yells, throbbed from the invisible black throats in the dark streets below and, "Hey, it's midnight!" voices called from the terrace, where we rejoined the party, everyone kissing and laughing and wishing each other "Happy New Year!"

As we held hands and swayed to the thin heartiness of "Auld Lang Syne," again the clanging rang out in the night . . .

Chapter 3

A HUNDRED AND EIGHT DEGREES FAHRENHEIT, THE YOUNG dominee who sat opposite me in the compartment assured me. I smiled and nodded wanly. How did he tolerate that dark flannel suit, the clerical collar? He looked unmoved, terrifically scrubbed, from his clear skin to the hair flattened on either side of an inflexible parting. Sweat prickled my own hair, pity I'd bothered to wash it, and it had looked so good . . . The firmly stuffed green leather seat stiffened me. The dominee and I were cooped up together and above his head was a display of vintage photographs: a rhinoceros in the game reserve, some Swazi warriors, a Reef town hall.

Outside, the dusty flat landscape seemed static, so featureless was it and so leisurely the train's progress through it. I sat, dazed, considering the deadliness of the prospect.

"How far are you going?" The dominee's voice roused me. He had the Afrikaner's blunt, thick-voweled accent with a lift on the last syllable. It sounded pleasant. Once I would have mocked it. I named the dorp. What if I added,

I'm going to the jail there, to see Paula Waszynski, a sabo-teur? That would shatter his sobriety! He was saying it was the stop after his parish. When I did not respond he opened a book . . . he had nice hands.

What did he think? That my dress was too short? He had certainly not looked at my legs. Though they were de-cently, uncomfortably, in stockings. I'd dressed formally in dark cotton, I'd even brought white gloves; Shula had teased, "Your cousin's influence?" but she treated the event casually, she was used to taking food and laundry to pris-oners; I was frankly scared, yet how could I refuse? You'd need the hide of a rhino to say "no" to Mrs. Warner—be-sides, one needed to be neighbourly—Paula's mother; I re-membered her long rigmarole about why she called herself Warner: in London, for a dressmaker, it was more suitable; people disliked refugees. But Paula was stubborn, had stuck to Waszynski even after she'd gone to live with an uncle, who owned a prosperous factory and was giving her a good education in Cape Town . . .

The train dawdled past a cluster of parched willows.

. . . Mrs. Warner—months ago yet I could still feel her clutch at my arm, she might have been drowning and I a tree . . . and those insatiable eyes . . . that cry, "What can I do to save my child? What got into her . . . that she should worry about those—those blacks! A good girl, she's a good student! Someone must have been at her, to do such a crazy thing!" She was unwilling, unable, to say "sabo-tage," shaking her head as if to clear it. "Paula forbids me to go myself to plead. Do you perhaps know Mr. Vorster? There was a picture, he looks a kind man. And Mrs. Vorster? She is a mother herself, surely she would understand a mother's suffering, a child's foolishness? What can I do?"

Some movement I made gave the dominee the impression I wanted a window opened. There was a rush of thick heat. At least, I said, this proved we were moving, which he thought amusing; anyway he laughed, and we decided stuffiness was preferable.

He was sweet when he laughed . . . Mrs. Warner's letter—the recollection set off a clamour of voices: hers, imploring, "Anne dear, perhaps Paula will listen to you, someone young like herself." And Alan Lemkovitz, warning, "Paula has absolutely rejected any appeal to the Minister, you'll have to be extremely tactful." Probably I was wasting time and nervous energy.

An insect buzzed distractedly inside the dominee's window. He put his book aside, lowered the window, then, hand cupped, edged the insect out and shut the window. I was laughing, he looked apologetic.

"No," I said, "sometimes if I see an insect on a path and think someone may trample on it, and I move it, afterward I get anxious, feel maybe I've interfered with its destiny."

"What if you were its destiny?" he said, then stopped as if he had made a daring joke which, given his Calvinism, perhaps it was. He quickly returned to his book.

Jakob Versfeld. The name sprang into focus. Of course, at the New Year's party someone had mentioned "Kobie" and I couldn't think who that was . . . What brought him to mind now? The dominee—because both were Afrikaners? Or Paula, the thought of jail, and my instinctive elation that this man, Kobie Versfeld, had said "no" to it?

He'd been on trial as a Communist—betrayed by a comrade —and had just vanished. Gone underground. A letter he had sent to the court declared that he would remain in the country, that he wanted to prove you could still oppose from within . . . news which rocked the country. I gazed heavy-lidded through the window. Far off a mirage shimmered, or were they real trees . . . Alan's voice, when I'd asked what he thought of Jakob Versfeld, sounded in my mind: "Kobie's a great man. Tragic error, though, his action—the harm it's done to his reputation. He was the only white man who could have united all races, all parties." What a hope, I thought sleepily . . .

I was jerked awake as a train rattled alongside ours. The dominee and I, from our empty compartment, looked out on the packed carriages, on black faces massed at the windows.

"Mineboys," the dominee said, his manner the precise courtesy of a native explaining to a tourist. "They're returning from their tribal area."

Like a herd of cattle, really, as in the mine compounds, a prize herd naturally. Earlier, when Shula was driving me to the station, we'd been held up by a long line of them in their customary progress through the city from compound to train, jogging single file, laden with trunks, strung-together cartons, pots, kettles, sewing machines, dressed in loud shirts and pants with jazzy patches and such hats! Ten-gallons were favourites. City Africans jeered and taunted but the line went doggedly on toward the station's non-white entrance. "That obedient trotting," Shulamuth had sounded pensive, "something . . . something castrated about it, hm?" Cattle, of course, had no concession store which could supply ten-gallon hats, owlish spectacles . . . what's known as fulfilling popular demand.

"You come from England, don't you?" asked the dominee.

I nodded. Partly I was too lazy to bother, partly I thought he'd be mistrustful if he knew I was indigenous, a "rooinek." For some reason, I rather wanted him to like me. He asked tentatively about my family—his name was Jan du Toit—and while I explained—that Mother had re-married since Father's death, that Lance was good at golf, that they lived now in Vancouver—I was thinking, if you knew how I was brought up to look down on, even loathe, your people, "die Volk." Odd, I'd rebelled against Father's anti-Semitism . . . Shulamuth was my best friend, and he would say, "But what do you see in her? She's so common, her father's in trade." But it wasn't that . . . no—not accurate. A Jew *and* in trade. When was it—it must have been the year Father died and I was fifteen—I'd shouted, "And what the hell's so superior about keeping chickens?" Of course we'd not known any Afrikaners apart from a few families like the Murrays, the Smits—Billy Theron too—who supported Smuts and so (it went without saying) were our own kind.

Against the stultifying drowsiness I welcomed the incentive of conversation. The dominee was touchingly proud of his mother. His father had gone off and left her and the children. "She has a boarding house in Bezuiden-hout Valley. That's a suburb of Johannesburg," he said. I felt gloom at the thought of the gone-to-seed neighbourhood, a decaying Colonial house, the boarders, low-paid white-collar workers . . . I could imagine his life: the struggle, deprivation, narrowness but, also, the devotion. I noticed his frayed cuffs, and his shoes—though they shone —had obviously been resoled more than once.

The train was slowing down, had stopped at a siding. A lone gum tree grew on the platform. Beyond a clutter of discarded railway trucks stood a lorry from which black men unloaded crates of Coca-Cola bottles. The train's hissing ceased. Voices died out, there was no other sound but the rattling of the bottles.

"Your father," said the dominee, "where . . ."

"He kept chickens," I said, and implied it was in England. I said I'd hated the wretched birds ever since and I dramatized the Saturday morning market, with chicken necks being wrung, their bodies leaping and jerking long after.

"He must have worked hard." The dominee's serious consideration rebuked facetiousness.

Father liked to tell Lance and me how he'd emigrated to bare veld and brought it to "orderliness." Orderliness. Dozens of chicken runs which gradually disintegrated. Outward manifestation—that's a thought, by God—of his spiritual and abdominal illnesses . . . "Dad's migraine," Mom called it.

"When he died," I said to the dominee, "I just couldn't cry. It became embarrassing, I pretended. And a few months later, when I killed a mouse by mistake, I couldn't stop . . . I never understood him."

"You were after all very young, a parent forgives much.

Of course," he smiled diffidently, "I only know from experience of my mother, and some parents in my parish."

But, I knew: I cannot ever retrieve . . . Quickly I continued: "When Father fought in the First World War he
was barely sixteen! He lied about his age . . ." The time
of his life, he adored talking about the trenches, and we
would groan, "Honestly, Dad, must you?" And in the
trenches he planned his dream farm, in all the danger and
mud he made drawings of chicken coops, they were
splotched with candle grease . . . When the farm—life
—didn't work out, he inflated patriotism, gentility, into a
faith. And drank. In a well-bred manner, of course. No
one could ever say we were common.

Outside all was silent now. It felt as if we would never
move again.

"Dad's migraine." Mommie . . . she'd forgotten to lock
the door . . . she was crying her eyes out . . . She took
shelter in anger: "Anne! Why aren't you ready, where's
your hat?" It was a Sunday . . . then gloved hand in
gloved hand we set out for church . . . the cocks crowed
near the canal . . . the canal's thin trickle . . .

The train gave a hesitant lurch, stopped again for a moment of suffocating stillness, and lurched on.

Perhaps we were all escaping from Father . . . and I
fortunate to be the younger and to have Grandpa,
contemptuous of his daughter's marriage and of Lance, lav-
ishing his elevated skepticism on me. No doubt he used me.
"Self-possession," he said, "as if you can ever possess your
self or anyone else, you who are born and die according to
a whim of nature, so that you are a tenant of a body with

that most precious of gifts, an intellect." And to Mom he'd say, "Louisa, for God's sake, go, put off holiness and put on intellect!"

How much did I express to the dominee? I was now wide awake, had almost ceased to feel crushed by the heavy heat. "I suppose I still feel remorse because Father died when I was at my most rebellious . . . I used to yell . . ." What he must have suffered, his anguish none the less real for being self-centered . . . once, twice, we'd looked deep into the soul of the other, seen a cruel, sad reflection of truth . . . indeed, am I not my father's daughter, with an aptitude for self-delusion?

The dominee allowed moments to pass, then, "It is not for us to say, but forgiveness, that was a promise . . ." He spoke confidently, but left the conditions unstated.

From the engine came a prolonged trumpeting. Goats scattered in bleating confusion into the veld. A white nanny became detached from the herd. Did it have yellow eyes, with black rims? The power of some half-forgotten memory touched me . . . how complicated to assess responsibility . . .

The dominee stood up. He opened the door and with a bashful expression went along the corridor.

I closed my eyes, let the rhythm of the wheels take over; I was not in a train that moved in a definite direction, but in a vacuum, gently jogging here and now which was nowhere, and no time. Perhaps neutrality of surroundings, the limbo-sensation, had enabled me to express—and to a stranger—things dormant or controlled . . . I felt again the choking, I drew a deep breath . . . heard again,

Father, "You'll be sorry when I'm gone." If he'd had his teeth in, but that munched-up crumbly look frightened me, I liked him crisp and handsome . . . my God! how sentimental could I get, he was a self-pitying egotist, let's face it. My anger was justified . . . Yes! That was the trouble . . . when Roger and I had quarreled I masked my fury, slithered into neutrality, a bloodless neutrality. I drove him mad. Why wouldn't I tangle? Because I didn't care enough? Yet often I thought: I want, I greatly desire, to say look, I believe I see into you, I'm sure you see into me, let's cut the crap, let us be and say what is, every instant, whatever is. Therefore, I determined: tonight, when you come in that door and say "Hi!" I shall look right into your eyes, be simply loving . . . And in the evening he came in the front door and it was all just like the night before only more so! With clarity I now could see: yes, I had not cared enough. Be "simply loving"? When, quite simply, I had not loved him.

The dominee came back to find me grinning to myself: struck belatedly and forcibly by the obvious, I felt an immense freedom, and when a steward came to inquire about lunch, I suggested, "Let's have a picnic in the compartment," and the dominee thought it a fine idea.

We ordered cold chicken, potatoes, and salad, with lager beer, and soon we were facing each other across the long table which the steward had unfolded from between the windows; as we ate and drank our meal became a celebration.

"Just like when we were kids," I said. "I loved long train journeys, and Dad organized us like an expedition. It was cozy. You know," I looked up from the drumstick I'd been nibbling at, "Father *was* forgiving."

The dominee nodded, smiling, then, "When I was a boy," he confided, "more than anything my dream was to become a great preacher, to be the instrument whereby the word penetrated men's hearts . . . do you think that is vanity?" He deprecated the idea with a laugh but clearly needed reassuring.

"Of course not, not with such a desire." And "Last year," I told him, "I was in Alabama and I heard a marvelous preacher, Martin Luther King."

The foreignness of the experience excited the dominee, and on his urging I described vividly how moved I was by King's noble words uttered in his sonorous rhythmic cadences, how afterward the huge crowd rose and stood, hand in hand, and I was hand in hand with two overalled workers, and we all sang, swaying in the way they do for this song, "We Shall Overcome," swaying and singing "black and white together I do believe we shall overcome someday."

Then Jan du Toit and I both laughed with exhilaration and no doubt the effects of the beer, and when we sobered down I remembered to add, "The only other whites there were two F.B.I. men." He looked impressed . . . so was I.

After a moment, "F.B.I.," he said, "that's the same as the Special Branch, isn't it?" I nodded. "There are some of them in our dorp, you know, they aren't very popular." I was glad to hear it. He let out a giggle. "One of them, the sergeant, he said to me the other day, 'Dominee du Toit,

33

what's wrong with me? When I go to the bioscope nobody comes and sits next to me.' " The memory made him giggle again. "Ach, makes you quite sorry for the man, though."

We made the most of it, you didn't often get the chance of a good laugh at them.

"I wish you stayed here . . . I mean right in the dorp," he said. And sounded reckless.

"Honger! Baas! Hungry! Missus?" The light shrill sound of children's voices cracked our happy mood as violently as a hammer aimed at a champagne glass. Kids, spindle-legged, pot-bellied, ran alongside the train, their hands fluttering. In the background were mud huts with big stones holding down the tin roofs. We were passing through a "black spot."

The dominee's eyes met mine. "It will not be long," he said hurriedly. "We are nearly there."

I felt muddled relief that there'd been no decision to make, our lunch was already cleared away . . . remembering how once Lance and I would toss out scraps and compete with each other in egging the piccanins on.

"There are some very terrible things." Painfully, now, Jan du Toit spoke. "Many thousands of Bantu families divided, the children and mothers made to live apart from the fathers. And when a child is told, your family is white, but you are coloured. No, but those things cannot be Christian." He shook his head and looked down sombrely while one hand moved restlessly as if to smooth out a crease in the cloth of his suit. "There are those in my church who feel a deep sorrow that our people do these things; we are but a handful. The brave ones, and you must understand the courage needed is very, very great, they have gone into the wilderness . . . they are threatened with excommunication. But a humble man like me, what can I do?" His eyes searched my face. "I am twenty-eight, I have only my matriculation . . . I could, with study, become a dominee in Holland. But this is my country. I try to do what is possible in my parish, we help the Bantu with blankets in winter. It is not that people are bad, but ignorant, and the politicians like to keep it that way, to use it . . ."

His translucent face laid bare his torment. He stood up suddenly and with a clumsy movement took his suitcase from the rack and put it by the door. He was frowning when he returned to his seat. "But think," he went on, "think what a hard job the police have; the Communists, the terrible trouble they make."

Quickly—it was a touchy subject—I asked, "But that lawyer who's gone underground, the Queen's Counsel, Jakob Versfeld, he sounds like a good man?"

"How could a man of such a family, a fine family, be deceived by such an ideology? I do not agree, however, with those who say he is a coward, that I do not accept. But lately, all the sabotage, that was criminal, wicked!"

Apprehensive that our tenuous contact could not survive, I spoke casually, "I've been told communism is rather beside the point, that mostly it was Africans demanding their rights—they tried so long by peaceful ways . . ." and, thinking of Paula, I added, "young white Liberals too."

But he had retreated, I could not reach him, implacable anger hardened his voice. "How does a man come to put a bomb in the station like that? Killing, maiming, innocent people—no! That I shall never understand. Never. Mad! He must have been mad."

The memory took me unawares, welled in me . . . I'd thought it happened at dawn, but not so, it was dark, and the cocks were crowing in the dark, when they hanged John Harris, by the neck, until he was dead.

My anger flared. "Your people! They've done atrocious things! How many have they killed, and got away with it . . . ?"

As if I'd hit him in the face.

The train was slowing down. His silence became a burden. Then, "Good-bye," he said, and offered me his hand.

Slowly the train moved on, leaving behind the dorp with its gray slate skimpy-spired church, the jerry-built garage, the brick and corrugated-iron houses, the wide desolate street, from which a small black boy in baggy shorts and red beret called and waved joyously at no one in particular.

Chapter 4

*P*AULA. THE THOUGHT COULD NO LONGER BE SHIRKED. IT was not the heat alone which had me wiping the palms of my hands. I was as nervous at the prospect of seeing her as I was of visiting the jail. Two or three times I had to go to the lavatory but the relief was short-lived.

I forced myself to itemize what I'd been told about her —her few friends had spoken with admiration, amusement, affection, or exasperation—she was a good student, she was obstinate, and proud of her name and race, with exceptional guts—it was Alan Lemkovitz who'd said how splendidly she'd stood up to ninety days. Unconventional, lonely, she had a sardonic sense of humour, or was she sarcastic and arrogant—this was a point of disagreement between Alan and his wife Jill, who had further opined that Paula was masochistic, and probably had sought imprisonment; after all, in jail you were relieved of any responsibility for apartheid. And—Jill's idiosyncratic view—"Paula tiresomely repudiates femininity."

But what brought her feelingly to life was Helen Mills's anecdote about the trio they had formed at university, with

Paula the flute, herself the pianist, and Milly, a fat girl, the violin. They'd had an absurd argument when Milly the violin asserted, "I put so much passion into my music and my politics because I've a passionate nature!"—with her plump arm raising her bow and pointing it accusingly at Paula—"Whereas you, you are so controlled!"—so that it sounded like a dirty word. "Excuse me!" Some fire was kindled in Paula. "I beg your pardon. I *have* passion! I do!" —almost attacking Milly, spitting out the words—"I *do* have passion! In my politics! In myself! You have not. Look at you! But I, I have had to learn control."

The train was slowing down. I braced myself.

I went by taxi to the jail. The front door intimidated. Carefully I tapped the knocker. Nothing happened. I tried again. A peephole opened. I said to the shadowed eyes, "I've come to see Miss Waszynski."

The door opened. A wardress, khaki-uniformed, a large key from a heavy bunch in her hand, let me in and locked the door behind me. I said, "Good morning." She indicated the visitors' book. "Purpose of visit"? I wrote: "Family matters." "Relationship"? What but "Friend." She led me down a corridor to a small room divided by wire mesh running through a high counter; at the counter a tall stool.

I was trying to settle on the stool when a young woman came in to the other side. Curious: she looked as if she belonged. She might well have worn such a dress outside. No one had prepared me for the brilliance of her black eyes.

She only glanced at me before looking away, and muttered a greeting. Her suspiciousness—however I'd prepared myself—shriveled such confidence as I still had. The assumption that our conversation was bugged, and the wardress near the door, didn't help.

"I think Alan Lemkovitz . . ." I began.

"What?"

Oh hell. The counter between us was so wide I was going to have to talk loud. I tried again, and told her of her mother being my neighbour in London. She nodded. Her expression gave nothing away. I found difficulty in keeping perched on the stool and leaned further forward to steady myself against the counter as I tried to express the depth of Mrs. Warner's feelings without the hysteria. Something must have echoed familiarly, however; an expression of sardonic irritation crossed Paula's face. I ended—the air was already electric with her ominous stillness—by conveying almost exactly her mother's message without referring directly to the Minister: "Your mother believes if you would allow her to appeal it would be possible to have your sentence considerably reduced, perhaps halved."

Her face was sullen.

Lamely I added: "You know, the offer, if parents . . ."

"My God! Will my mother never learn, never understand!" Her voice, low at first, turned rough with despairing rage. She must have guessed the moment she had had Alan's message, what I was coming for, been boiling with it, and now the lid was off. "Yes! If the parents come and grovel, and beg forgiveness, and say their child sinned and is sorry. Je—!" She stopped herself as the wardress eyed her.

She gave a slight shake of her head as if to clear her thoughts. For the first time I was reminded of her mother.

"It's business as usual," she said. "Like those Jews who gave that gold medal to Malan. She just can't see. Won't see . . . what makes it worse, from what bits of news we get here, only the whites are being released. And Abel—you know—who's coloured, got the longest sentence of us all. . . . Tell her no!"

"I understand. I'll write, make it quite clear but try to be tactful." And to ease Paula's pain I made meaningless remarks about her mother looking well. "And you? How are things?" I asked. "And how the hell do you manage to stick on these damn stools?"

That did it, that ridiculous cry of discomfort propitiated her. Her face unbuttoned. "If it weren't for our studies," she said, "we'd go out of our minds! Especially for me the philosophy . . . you know I've come across Marcus Aurelius. I understand he has fallen from grace, being too stoical, but he has shown me how it is in my power to retire into myself, sort of find freedom there, you know? Sometimes, even inside the cell, I can again be walking along that beach at Camps Bay—you know that part?—between the rough sea and the mountains. He is right, the universe *is* transformation." She stopped.

"I'd like to read him."

She went so far as to grin. "There now! And he was such a modest man he thought his name would be short-lived."

With the abatement of anger her voice had slowed down. "You know, sometimes"—her confidence was growing—"one of us gets in a bad depression. That pulls us all down. But sometimes, for no reason, you feel hopeful . . . as if the world is smiling."

She made a gauche gesture, half smiled, and I realized just how shy she must be. Something struck a chord—her eyes, the carelessly cut hair, her Jewishness, what she had said. "Have you read Simone Weil at all?" I asked.

"No?"

"She was French, a Jew, in the Resistance. A philosopher." I told a bit about her books, that they might be relevant, if often incomprehensible, to me anyway; that she'd been very neurotic—so what—she'd had genius, and that she'd died not long ago. Paula asked me to try and get one of her books sent in, then talked of Alan with respect and affection. I said how warmly he'd spoken of her and of her courage in ninety days . . .

She said, "I only must hope my experience *then* can be of help to others." And added—I had to stretch forward, her voice was so low—"At least, now, there is nothing to fear." She was not looking at me. It was true; the passion was there, under most strenuous control.

The wardress announced time was up. As I was about to withdraw Paula called me back. "Please, Anne Dawson, I'm sure you will try to soften the blow for Mother. I know she is thinking of me. I should not get so furious. Poor Mother, all she wanted for me was to make a nice home."

The jail door closed behind me. "A nice home"—her mother's words when she'd thrust the notebook on me. There was not much to it, a handful of densely scribbled notes. Paula must have got rid of it and mailed it to her mother when the police began to arrest the students. "Perhaps you will understand, Anne," Mrs. Warner had said. "I do not. Why does Paula rake up all that old stuff? It is dead. Finished. Why does she not leave it alone? Marry some nice boy, make a nice home . . ."

NOTEBOOK—PROPERTY OF P. WASZYNSKI

In Auschwitz, Sonderkommando No. 12 were the only Jews who fought back against their torturers, against the murderers of all the previous Sonderkommandos. By fighting back they *used* their deaths. No waste. 853 deaths that meant something. Useful deaths. Against how many millions that were meaningless? The lemmings. The millions who went like lemmings to be gassed. Why? Because *"Business as usual"* was their mentality. (Nyiszli paperback)

"The persecution of the Jews was aggravated, slow step by slow step, when no violent fighting back occurred." (Bettelheim)

Must not happen again! Jewish acceptance of degradation maybe gave the SS the idea Jews would go meekly to the gas chambers.

Resignation is peculiar to our race, that creature, that Jewish doctor, Nyiszli, says. No No No!

The torturer needs to create guilt in the prisoner. Jews willing. The guilty tribe?

From what experience did our forefathers pray: "Thou hast chosen us from all peoples, Thou hast loved us and taken pleasure in us"? From what dark well of self-deceiving did we accept that we were "chosen," thence that our guilt was the heavier?

How many innocents walked naked into the gas chambers, comforting themselves with: "We have committed abomination, we have gone astray." My God, religion corrupts! Innocence corrupts!

We scapegoats bring upon us anti-Semitism by our very abjectness. Israel is not the answer, but to find self-respect wherever we may be. To insist, but not assert. To say No!

Ghastly story that man told at that awful party, of the Jew who owned a big hardware store who said to him, "Isn't it the most wonderful thing, the local golf club *invited* me to apply for membership?" And this man replied, "No, you've earned it. Through your humanity." And telling me how the Jew had tears in his eyes!

Ghastly party. Why do I go? Always the same.

It is for the Sonderkommando that I must act. How they inspire! It is unthinkable that they should not have existed. This world would be out of the question, utterly intolerable, had there only been the SS and creatures like Nyiszli . . . Jesus! when they drove, with guns and dogs, "a living chain" of naked men and women—and children, dear God—into the great ditches filled with fire. Five to six thousand a day. And Nyiszli says he agrees with Mengele: after the pyres the crematorium is "a place where one could live in a pretty decent way."

Why do I often feel like a cur, anticipating being kicked?

Today is March 21. Sharpeville Day. And it is Bach's birthday. Sharpeville . . . Jesus! that photograph of them still laughing as they are shot in the back, shot dead . . . after they have made their protests against the pass laws. Men and women and children. "Have mercy upon me,

43

my bones are consumed." "Tis your hour now, ye dread powers of darkness." St. Matthew Passion says it all.

How to be efficient? I'm such a muddle. Not good enough to mean well. Even passion is not enough. Discipline!

Sorel wanted the ashes stirred to make flames leap. To be alive, only alive, alive unto the end. (Pasternak) That's my desire. Because I'm *not* alive. Is suffering proof of life? How can you measure suffering unless you've experienced bliss?

To see people happy. That is beautiful. That young couple watching the squirrels in the Gardens. How I want people to be happy, to feel for each other.

Johannesburg. Staying with Helen, horrid experience— walking from Parkview bus after sunset, African tried to grab my bag and I felt something sharp prod my spine, thought—this is it!—when people suddenly came out of a gate and he just vanished. Nightmare thought—tsotsis kill and cripple more and more thousands in townships. Will the struggle ultimately be between anarchistic black gangsters and white neo-Nazis?

Today I was waiting for the bus in town, a barefoot shriveled kid was begging, hands cupped together in customary manner. I gave something to him and got on bus. As we drove off saw two hefty men get hold of him, cursing and hitting him with their fists and no one protesting and I unable to move as we speeded away. More dreadful than wild beasts. What is to be done . . .

Camus: "If we are to fail, it is better in any case to have stood on the side of those who choose life than on the side of those who are destroying." And—"We think

44

we are dying of grief and yet life wins out." We must do what is necessary "so that life for all will again be possible with all."

Aim of rebellion is to transform. How to rebel without becoming destructive? *The* question: how to cease to be victims without becoming executioners?

Self-respect. To the rebel this matters more than life.

Freedom. Justice. How I've accepted these without thought and only now see them to be clichéd slogans. A balance between them, the only reasonable aspiration?

Mystic virtue of "the people"—can there be virtue simply in being oppressed, poor? Can it be true that "victims" quickly become a bore? Surely not.

Mother would say, "You should find yourself a nice boy, then you could make a nice home." Poor Mother. She would despair if she knew! As if I was not awkward enough before. People are daring, generous, to embark on relationships. I wear armour. Yet marriage can be so beautiful. Alan and Jill just after the twins born—the family made a full circle. But hard for a woman, the man's passion for his work. I would be jealous, would want to be in his work as well as in his home. Is that greedy? Possessive? Besides, look how Jill is no longer political!

Louis Trichardt case: white farmer who beat black labourer to death. The "labourer"? Twelve years old, weight a hundred pounds. The farmer, sentenced to five years. 2,000 neighbouring farmers promptly petition for his release, express distress at the suffering *his* family must endure if he is jailed!

"If today Negroes in Africa march against the guns of a police that defends apartheid—even if hundreds of them will be shot down and tens of thousands rounded up in concentration camps—their march, their fight will

sooner or later assure them of a chance of liberty and equality." (Bettelheim, Foreword, page 12)

Danger collective. Responsibility individual. We must use what tools we have—what tools we are—we can not, must not, sit by in apathy. Indifference equals support of Verwoerd and Vorster. Apathy led to the Nazis' gas chambers. To be indifferent is to condone. Worse! It is to collaborate. What is the moral distinction between the doctor who cut up his fellow Jews, who dissected two-year-old twins, *knowing* they'd been killed specially, knowing knowing KNOWING, and Hitler and the SS who ordered the experiments? Where draw the line between Jews here who gave a gold medal to the Prime Minister, and the farmer who beats a labourer to death? Between Verwoerd and the English-speaking businessmen who whitewash apartheid? Business as usual!

At long last—to act! Against cruelty, against injustice, against Master Race bigotry. Knowing there will be no harm to any human being. To act! Fear, yet—what? Exaltation? The putting away of self-consideration. Becoming part of all those others.

The sole object of revolution is the abolition of senseless suffering. Do all revolutions inevitably increase suffering at first?

Dostoievsky's *The Possessed*—is this what we resemble?

Alas, *here* what are we? Show-offs? Yet where else find *action?*

Chapter 5

DELICIOUS, AFTER A DUSTY AFTERNOON DOWNTOWN, TO sit in a pavement café drinking iced coffee while the air grows cooler with the approach of evening . . . in the background the convulsive surge of after-office traffic, and beneath the flicker of neon signs the pavements alive . . . Outside the Portuguese delicatessen Indians selling oranges, grapefruit, flowers; accents mingling—Indian, German, Scots. A group of black men in dark flannel suits, keen shoes and hats, bantering together as they head with idle deliberation, taut-shouldered, for the Gents' Outfitters, clustering there, not far from my table, to consider the window display . . . a small-waisted white girl in short shorts passes them . . . they cast no glance nor audible comment. And if they had? The things one never used to question . . . pants and bras carelessly left lying around for Amos to tidy. A fat black girl is shuffling by, dusty-shoed, sulky, weary . . . one of the men calls after her, she tosses her head, slogs on . . . his friends mock him, their voices rising bawdily. A muscular white man in a hurry collides with him, shoves him rudely aside to stalk on . . . "Fuckin' white baas," the black spits after him. And turns in ribald laughter to his friends.

I feel clear, sharp, alive. I study my suntanned arm, stretch a long leg, have a slow sip of coffee, and hear again Shula's "Oh, Cookie, it's so *awful* here. But I couldn't live anywhere else . . ." The evening when Jacob was very late from school . . . the slam of a door, a whiff of chalk dust, and, "Where have you been, Jake?" she was greeting him before she realized he was in tears. His tough impishness eclipsed, he let her gather him into her arms, wheedle from him: the kids at school had called him a Commie. "What did you say?" I asked. "That it's not true, that we're Liberals!"

"Come and help me unpack!" I urged. "And show me which are my towels . . . I'm sharing your bathroom; you know I've moved from my cousins'?"

"Oh good! Are you going to live with us always?" And so I'd settled in with the Lowens.

Ben and Shula, their meeting—how many years ago, could it be ten? It was winter, our second term at university; she and I were basking in the sun on the steps of Great Hall in a break between lectures and beyond her I saw this solid young man with an armful of books hurtling down so that my warning as she chanced to move into range came too late. Literally they bumped into each other, literally fell in love at first sight, even I had the sensation that time hesitated . . . brainy Shula shiningly happy and Ben—though we couldn't yet know how remarkable this was and thought it was simple embarrassment—utterly silent.

"Cameriere!" From the table next to mine a young man

clicks his fingers and calls again, "Waiter!" considering my form as he does so. Nostalgia pervades me—for a small restaurant on the Via Appia . . . beyond the pines, olive trees and poppies and yellow daisies, while cicadas clamour in the summer heat . . .

". . . it's so awful here . . ."

Ben and Shula . . . if, like me, like so many others, they'd left, what would their lives be now? In London, say. Shula, concerned with prisoners' welfare or mental health? Not unlike her work here for wives of political prisoners but with some element of hope. And Ben? A political columnist with virtually interchangeable targets: Wilson, Heath, Johnson, Nixon. They'd live in a small house near Swiss Cottage, making the most of its intellectual life—the theater club, the concerts and political lectures—Ben would take the children to Hampstead Heath on Sundays while Shula cooked the dinner. They'd be a lively family living where their beliefs were the accepted norm. Beliefs which, here, were abused, and their lives made into a long-drawn-out drama in which by the nature of their integrity they played modestly heroic roles.

They had survived . . . at what price: survival? Sharpeville, the shootings . . . Five years ago now but springing fresh the shock, the horror, the hope . . . Hope? Yes, as the outrage of the world mounted, with Westminster, Washington, Moscow moved to severe censure, and with the economic crisis thereby precipitated, then had come the unbelievable moment of hope! Africans marched and the Government faltered, slackened its grip, revoked the pass laws . . . the breakthrough at last? To change, to decency. And then . . . business as usual: Johannesburg, Wall Street, the City of London, solidarity asserted. Business as usual and thousands imprisoned. Arousing a dreadful despair . . . even in Ben. One would expect alcohol to heighten his hilarity, that he'd clown his way to insensibility, but with his head bowed he drank, shut away from and suspicious of friends . . . Shula's agonized, "But we love each other, you'd think love could break through wouldn't you . . . wouldn't you?" while with dumb faith she tried to cope. "Melancholia," the psychiatrist said, somewhat obviously—Ben only saw him to appease Shula, he had no intention of being helped.

"But I couldn't live anywhere else."

With a long spoon I scoop whipped cream from the surface of the coffee, and savour it.

For three years . . . until . . . when Mandela, Makhana, the others, were arrested, Ben stopped drinking. "Just like that, Cookie," Shula put it, in retrospect. "Well, no . . . a terrific act of will. But he has no illusions today. None."

Ben . . . his little joke, "It's being so cheerful keeps me fit." Life was peppered with comic happenings—what he called the bumbledum of local bureaucracy and ministerial *faux pas*—each Sunday his column was fiercely funny, week after week exposing disgraces. "Why do you think those bastards in the Government let people like me keep at it? Because they know ruddy well we're no real threat, and to the outside world they say 'Look at our great free press! What a democracy we are!' "

My hand encircling the glass feels chilled. I rub until it

tingles . . . and remember last night, heading home with Shula and the children. She was resisting their demands for chocolates, "No more now! We're nearly there and it's suppertime!" when under a streetlight loomed the huddle of men, four black men handcuffed together and, with them, two policemen. I glimpsed one face in close-up, raw-boned, desperate, then a policeman grabbed him and shook him like a bundle.

"Charlie!" shouted Jake. "Ma, they've got Charlie!"

A moment's pandemonium before Shula stopped the car, told us to wait there, got out, slammed the door . . . with the kids peering from the windows, then Shula hurrying, stumbling in the dark, a pick-up van pulling up, Shula re-monstrating, a policeman's voice rising: "No use, lady, he's under arrest." And her low voice, "But he told you, his pass is in his room, we're just outside the gate." "Lady, there's nothing I can do . . . normal procedure . . ." The men being jostled into the van, locked in, driven away.

Shula was back with us, telling the children it was noth-ing serious, Charlie had left his pass again and she would have to bail him out. There was nothing to worry about. "Cookie, let them each choose a chocolate, just one."

With the children safe in bed, she let go: "This bloody country, I'm sick to death of the bloody bloody place!

"But I couldn't live anywhere else."

A loud hooting from the street . . . an African youth in studded leather jacket sidles contemptuously through the fast-moving traffic. Along the pavement an effeminate man pushes a pram while a big-bosomed blonde in baby-doll dress castigates him in Afrikaans.

Those huddled men, the raw-boned face . . . was there ever a time when it hadn't happened?—policemen accosting, interrogating, demanding passes, handcuffing, hustling off—there must have been a time, surely. No, I cannot recall . . .

This morning, an age ago, Shula and I were sitting on the public bench in the dingy courtroom, and in the cage outside crowded with Africans there was a conspicuous lack of laughter. A white-haired bland man entered the court: the Bantu Commissioner, for whom we rose. A black interpreter lounged against the dock. Two or three petty officials sat about. No one appeared to notice us, yet there was the sense of being observed.

Shula's purple velvet toque was calculated to intimidate the toughest official, so she'd said before we set out, when I'd gazed transfixed. Then, when my eyes met hers, we'd collapsed in helpless giggles. Now the sight of it left me dull.

An order is given and from the cage comes a tall unshaven man, Number One, accused of altering a date in his "reference" book. The Commissioner asks: "Guilty or not guilty?" The man says earnestly that when he was discharged from his job his master wrote the wrong date in his pass book; he therefore corrected it. "A serious matter," says the Commissioner, bored. "Two rand or seven days." Thump of a rubber stamp.

Number Two is in the dock: thin, raggedly dressed, sullen, holding an obstreperous orange hat. He says he has lost his book. "Sixteen rand or eight weeks." Thump.

An aggressive-looking man, behind his defiance, apprehension. Numbers Four, Five, Six . . . how long for each trial? One minute? Two?

At home, when the rest of the family were out or too busy, from the time I had learned to write well enough Amos and Cornelius would come to me: "Can I have a night pass, please, nonnie?" Then I would spell out on a piece of paper: *Please pass native Cornelius* with the curfew time, our address, the date. And I would sign my name.

Number Thirteen is in the dock, a boy, very frightened. He says something timidly, is told to speak up. "I was working in the school holidays." He bows humbly. He is under sixteen. He goes free.

Free.

A booklet—scraps of paper—what's your name? Who's your boss? Have you paid your taxes? A word, a figure out of place? It's not in your pocket? Ten rand or five weeks. Sixteen rand, eight weeks. In jail, a criminal, striped vest and shorts, head shaven, barefoot. Humiliate. Degrade. Emasculate. Thump of rubber stamp. Women as well— Two rand, seven days. The children? That's their look-out. Their mothers shouldn't be so careless. "*Kaffermeid, waar's jou pas?*" God almighty! And we a part of it, sitting here, witnessing, pitying, feeling brave for having come. Patronize. Emasculate. Never have I felt so white, so middle class, so "privileged," so guilty. Paula's note: "Jesus! that picture of them still laughing as they are shot in the back, shot dead." Sharpeville, this, *this* is what they protested about, those men, those women, those children . . .

53

Number Twenty-five: very young, shabby. "Guilty or not guilty?" He fumbles in his pocket, brings out the booklet. The police had not asked for it. "Case withdrawn."

Number Thirty: Charlie! He does not see Shulamuth, being wholly intent on the process. A good-looking young man, usually cocky. Now uneasy. Shula is smiling brightly, I find I am too. Cheer up, Charlie, your madam and her chum have come to rescue you!

Charlie explains he carelessly forgot his pass in his room, went a few hundred yards to the shops, was rounded up on his way back, told the police but they would not . . . "Ten rand or five weeks."

As he turns to leave the dock he sees us; Shulamuth nods hard, we go at once to the office to pay the ten rand, Shulamuth making voluble complaint to the clerk against the police and the system, yet remaining courteous.

Outside again we did not speak, only cast off our respectable headgear.

Sometimes the blacks passing by the pavement café would look at us whites relaxing with our cold drinks; mostly they ignore us. Neon signs flash brighter as the sunset fades . . .

54

Chapter 6

*A*LAN LEMKOVITZ SWIVELLED HIS CHAIR SLIGHTLY, SO
that the lamp on his desk no longer intruded between
us and, attentive, waited for me to explain.

"Alan, do you think people can still be useful here? I
mean in so hopeless a situation?"

At once I regretted my framing of the question, it
sounded patronizing. Besides, I was wasting his time with
imprecision, valuable time when he was leading the defense
in a new political case, though when I'd asked to see him
he'd been reassuring: of course he could fit me in. But, as he
regarded me quietly, I was aware again of the empathy I'd
first experienced on New Year's Eve, and believed now he
would understand my need.

"Perhaps," he said, "I should tell you about something
which happened a few months ago. Jill and the twins had
gone down to her family in Natal and I set off alone, driving round the coast, camping out anywhere, wherever I
chose, and you know, Anne, I had the feeling of falling in
love with this country. A most definite sensation. One day
I fished from a beach going on for miles and miles. There

was no other human being . . . far away I could see cliffs and forests . . . I stayed there tussling, hour after hour, sometimes getting a catch, a barracuda once, you know? I felt like a small scrap of humanity in the wilderness. And I suddenly saw, more sharply than ever before, into the inadequacy of my work . . . that I was dealing with a couple of nerve ends in a body riddled with cancer."

He paused. He seemed to pursue an ambiguity. "But this feeling about the country, the intense sensual feeling, was somehow bound up in . . . made possible by, the nature of my work, and I realized too that the work has to be done. There is no alternative. As obvious as that."

Wryly he added, "I'm afraid that's not much of an answer to your question."

"I think you've answered me." I hesitated, then asked, "Do you know of anything I might do?"

He looked delighted. "Come with me," and he was opening his door, ushering me out, down the corridor, up some stairs, into another group of advocates' chambers where he stopped at a door, knocked, poked his head in, asked, "Matt, have you a moment?" and I found myself in a room lined with law books, where a redheaded man worked at a brief-strewn desk.

"Matthew Marais," said Alan. "And this is Anne Dawson, who wrote the article I showed you on the pass-law courts."

He rose to shake hands, his grip was cool and spare.

"Anne's offered to be useful," Alan went on. "What do you think, Matt?"

56

His eyes, dark in a thin, lined face, fixed mine, assessing. "How much time have you?" The voice was abrupt, markedly accented. "What is immediately needed would occupy you pretty well full-time."

I heard my voice say, positively, "That's all right." Hastily repossessed myself to add, "Naturally I must be able to continue my writing, to earn . . ."

"Good." Enthusiasm glimmered. His hands, slightly freckled with reddish hairs just visible at the wrists, were laid palm down, flat on the desk. "The survey, then?" he questioned Alan.

"Exactly." Alan was satisfied. "Well, if you don't mind, I'll leave you to fill in." And, patting my shoulder encouragingly, he departed.

"Immensely valuable, your offer," Matthew Marais said. For the first time he smiled, an oddly gay smile for a mouth that had seemed grim. "We urgently need a survey of the scores of political trials over the past two to three years, both for our own use and for law associations overseas. It's a question of analyzing evidence, cross-referencing witnesses, and so on. A massive job, and of course a continuing one. It means sending out regular installments. Unfortunately I can't explain more now, I've got to be in court. When would suit you?"

I was surprised to find the curt interview had exhilarated me. "Tomorrow morning?"

"Good."

He was putting papers into a briefcase and said he must get on. I said I was parked near the Magistrate's court, actually, and, as I spoke, I suddenly realized who he was. I'd met his wife once, Joyce . . . Communists, so one understood.

He was saying, "We can go together."

I hesitated. They must keep a close watch on him . . . probably tailed. What could be amusing him?

"Right," I said.

We came out of the building into streets strident with traffic. As we threaded our way along the crowded pavements the wind freakishly flicked our faces with powdery dust. He moved lazily but covered the ground fast. I had to hurry to keep up. As we were passing a towering new building complex, a white foreman shouted at blacks unloading a truck. I felt exhilaration ebb in the plaguey atmosphere as I tried to keep pace with the preoccupied angular man beside me. A scrap of newspaper settled against my ankle and took an effort to shake off. The sun had gone in. Clouds bulked. We had to wait for a traffic light. As he watched it impatiently, "You'll soon get the hang of the job," he said, "once you've studied some of the court records. The vital task," he continued when the green light released us and we strode on, "is to expose what is going on in the Eastern Cape. Something peculiarly atrocious . . ." His next words were lost in the crackle and flash of thunder and lightning as rain pelted down. He drew me into a doorway where we waited. I felt vaguely hostile, his expectations weighed on me . . . What the hell had I let myself in for . . . Alan should have given me more time. The heavy shower quickly emptied the streets of all but cars which swooshed by, windshield wipers frantic, and African delivery " boys " pedalling on, their bicycles swaying as they strained against the force of the downpour.

I felt rather than saw his restlessness as he glanced at his watch. How, I was wondering, how on earth does an intelligent man accept the jargon, "revisionism," "hyenas," I mean really. At which my ragbag mind tossed up a scrap: Athanasius reviled heretics as "wolves" and "cuttlefish." A grin hovered between my mind and my mouth. His gaze was on me. Something in him exposed the superficial, induced respect.

"About the Eastern Cape," I said, "did you want to suggest anything particular?"

His smile again took me by surprise.

"If you could get down there," he said, "do for those trials, taking place in obscurity, what you did on the pass courts . . . a fine article, that."

I felt ridiculously pleased.

"Come on," he said, "the rain's over."

In fact it was still drizzling, but now I found our walk enjoyable, the atmosphere clear. We crossed a street and came to an arcade of musty secondhand shops and cheap jewellers; we passed a dilapidated doorway. " That," he said, "is where the African miners' strike was organized back in '46."

His laconic words in telling me about that time could not disguise the potency of the recalled experience, and when he left me at Shula's car, my imagination was dilated . . . as I drove home I could see him, a thin-faced redheaded youth, tensed over a duplicating machine, churning out leaflets till three and four in the morning, helping the black miners, with Indians too, and other whites . . . laughing with elation at a job done and the risks ahead, all piling into old motorcars and driving miles to the mines to distribute, to urge the strikers to hold on . . . hold on! Seventy thousand of them out! Seventy-five thousand! Ten shillings a day, their demand. Panic headlines . . . Yes, now I could remember . . . Father: "The natives have risen!" and in the darkness our fear. Then, with morning, fresh headlines, and: "No need to panic. Smuts has the situation in hand, thank God!" Smuts, the companies, called out the police, called out the troops to shoot down the strikers . . . with bayonets and truncheons the miners were driven back to the rock face. Their union was outlawed, strikes were outlawed . . . never again would they organize . . .

When I got home I told Shula that I had a job. She was excited and said we'd celebrate; anyway she'd promised the kids a braai, and Alan and Jill were coming; she'd invited Matt as well, only as usual he was too busy.

After tea we settled down on the terrace to mend cushion covers. The cat stretched dozing in the sun.

I thought it best to air my mild misgivings about Matthew Marais's politics, thus dispelling them, but Shula's face and my own ears told me how ineptly I did so and I ended up laughing. "Yes, Shula, I *do* know!" as she scoffed, "Dubious about Matt, you *are* a nut!"

She reminded me of Professor Gibbon's parable of the few who broke out of the Cave. Matt, she said, was one of those—a strong, independent Afrikaner. She didn't believe he was actually a Party member, and she peered belligerently at me. I was not used to her spectacles and couldn't help grinning, which undermined the sagacity of my comment that since the Communist Party was illegal, I didn't see how she could know who was or wasn't a member. "Anyway," I said to mollify, "I can imagine he's a good lawyer." Then couldn't resist adding, "That dry, intimidating manner."

"Matt intimidating! You're joking!"

"Oh, Shula dear, I do love you. Of course I was . . . But no, now I come to think of it, it's true, he did intimidate me!" The idea made us both laugh.

And while she told me that it was Matthew more than any other friend who had helped her through the three years of Ben's alcoholism, we could hear from down below the lawnmower as Charlie drove it back and forth . . . we could smell the freshly cut grass. I squinted into the eye of my needle and steadied the thread through, seeing again the blunt-cut red hair, the heavily lined face—yet he must be well under forty—the crooked nose and changeable mouth, eyes that disconcerted . . . "You didn't mention his wife, when you said you'd invited him . . ."

"Didn't you know? Joyce ran off to Rhodesia with some man . . . she was quite incapable of being faithful."

"When I met her she was having an affair with Henry Thomson."

"I thought Matt was well rid of her but he was hopelessly in love. He's shut women out ever since. Of course, he works so darned hard, that's a protection. Helen Mills now, she was dead keen, we always invited them together, but the moment he realized how she felt, he withdrew absolutely. Does that surprise you?"

"I don't know . . . No." If he had loved unreservedly . . . unconditionally . . . The lawnmower buzzed on, back and forth.

I changed the subject. "What's Henry Thomson like now? I mean, does he still take political cases?"

"Good gracious! Henry! A pillar of respectability, or should I say a monument of ego!"

"I must say, he was always sweet to Grandpa . . . he used to play polo with Patrick . . ." I was remembering from my impressionable teens a mocking golden-brown face, shoulders rippling under the white sweat shirt, as he rode toward us and slid from his horse to greet the family.

"I dare say," Shula remarked. "He's got charm enough for six."

"It amazes me," I backtracked, "that there are so *few* Communists."

Shula put down her sewing and stared into the distance toward the northern hills. "I envy them their dedication, their certainty. You know, Cookie, it's as though my mind's involved, and my heart, but somehow not my very being." I felt the sorrowfulness of her admission. "Trouble is," she gave a short laugh, "as I've told you before, I couldn't live anywhere else."

Yes . . . "What a bore that it matters," I said, "one's politics."

"Nonsense!" Ben was back from the office. "What matters is goodies and baddies."

"What matters right now, lovie," Shula said as she collected the cushions, "is that you and Charlie get things ready for the braai."

A soft dark night, with the Milky Way like a drift of smoke among the brilliant stars and planets. The acrid fragrance of charcoal, meat and ash lingered. Jacob and his sisters said good night over and over again, their voices diminishing across the lawn until, after a last chorus from the terrace, a door closed on them.

"Peace at last," sighed Shula. "Come on, let's drink to Anne's new job."

Contentment . . . with Ben, Shulamuth, Alan and Jill . . . Jill—perhaps one could seldom have equal affinity with both husband and wife, perhaps her impeccably groomed elegance gave an impression of coldness. Sometimes I felt she was not quite real, perhaps it was because she'd come so far from her own people . . . at all events, tonight we'd got each other into better focus; our mutual wariness was dissipated. Now she said, "Improbable, surely, Anne, that you won't miss London. How is it, these days, living there?" Her question, like a pebble dropped into a pool, cast its implications . . . it seemed she still hankered, despite the tough determination that had carried her through her rebellion against family—Natal British, wealthy, in sugar—and against her background—a snob school near Ascot and the deb routine of a London season—to marry Alan, his grandfather an itinerant trader in the Kimberley diamond rush, his father a furniture manufacturer. Alan, a Jew. Alan, who also awaited my reply.

"I don't know why," I said lightly, "the question always brings out a rash of clichés . . . swinging, but all passion spent. You never see enough of the people you care about —but intellectual compensations, civility . . . You see what I mean!"

"While I long to go back!" She laughed at the waste of it, and tapped a cigarette nervously against the packet from which she'd extracted it. "So many people have left, we've got more friends there than here. It's easier for the men," she did not look at Alan, "much easier. Their work means everything to them . . ." Alan's hand brushed against the unfairness of the remark but he let her talk on. "I'm afraid, now," she said, "afraid to make friends because you lose them so fast, you become too damn vulnerable!" The last word exploded in protest.

"I do see," I said. "Of course it's easy for me. I suppose London's the safest, the most rational place there is. Only I find it hard to get excited about anything there. It's curious, there's some quality about life here—maybe it's all of you, perhaps in spite of one's self, roots do matter—I feel more alive here." I was sure that Alan, at any rate, knew exactly what I meant.

"My God," said Jill, "all I can say is, you must thrive on tension."

"That's natural," Alan defended. "When we're faced with a problem, we generate energy to try to solve it."

"We do?" she spoke with exaggerated languor.

Ben soothed the fractious moment with a quick, "You're both right," and moved to replenish our drinks while Shula asked, what about the States, she remembered a letter in which I'd said I felt terrifically alive in New York . . .

"The States? The love/hate relationship of all time! Drives me mad but fascinates, some wonderful people, and then weird reminders of this place. The white Southerners, for one thing. In New York I saw a play by James Baldwin, critics complained that his Southern whites were caricatures, but it's true, they nearly always are! Here too, even with Patrick and Sally and their friends, you know?"

Shula nodded and Ben—he never had liked Patrick—remarked, "Don't I know!"

"Majorca last year, remember, darling?" Jill said to Alan. "The Wentworths and those other English couples . . . before, they would have been in Kenya, now they're colonizing the Mediterranean, getting away from their dreadful Labour Government, the dreadful taxes, the lack of servants, talking like characters in a Somerset Maugham novel."

Shula, as she poured out the coffee, said she supposed it was inevitable, after all you were only half alive once you turned your back on reality.

Those were exactly the people, I said, who panicked about the "black danger" and "agitators." "And when I was in the South a Negro leader—a moderate—was shot in the back by a white man who everyone said would not be convicted, and who wasn't. Before I left, three children were killed when a white threw a bomb into a Sunday school. I got to feeling bloody sick at being white."

No one spoke for a while, then, "All the same," said Ben,

"I'd like to go to the States. I inquired once about jobs there, but nothing doing." So, they had thought of coming away . . . but of course . . .

Shula said, without warning, "Anne needs reassuring about Matt." And smiled sweetly at me.

I blinked reproachfully back. Overeagerly I explained: "It's not that I mind about communism. In Europe, after all, it's old-hat; only Spain and Portugal imprison them as they do here . . . of course, my family were madly prejudiced . . . I guess it brushed off on me . . . the anxiety that if you work with them, they'll use you . . . you know?"

Alan treated my difficulty with respect. "There are some liberals who remain adamant but others among us feel the situation's far too grave to maintain such divisive attitudes . . . political beliefs are irrelevant . . . you work with those you trust . . ."

"When we were in prison together after Sharpeville, we knocked along tolerably well," Jill began, when I interrupted, "But I didn't know you'd been . . ." "No," she was smiling, "it's not something I go on about, after all, I'd done nothing splendid or dramatic, I'd only been civil to some of the demonstrators who happened to be clients of Alan's." She broke off for Alan to light her cigarette and their faces became complementary parts fused by the glow of the match, his somber, gentle, hers aquiline, unusually animated . . . she exhaled and turned back to me. "Well, we were crowded into a huge cell, mostly Communists, a couple of Liberals, and me who was, so to speak, nothing at all . . .

and of course there were tensions, the odd blow-up . . . I couldn't stand one woman, Georgina Kaye—perhaps you've met her in London?—and doubtless she thought me a snob . . . but I'm sure it was as much that we are a bunch of neurotics as a question of clashing ideologies."

"The bogey's so exaggerated, the result is the Communists get credit for everything!" Shula exclaimed. "Anyway, in a sensible country most of them would simply be social democrats, right? For donkeys' years the C.P. was the only party which accepted non-white members. And that explains a lot . . ."

"There you go, puss, generalizing . . ."

"Oh, Ben, I like *that!* And you with your goodies and baddies!"

"As I was about to say, Marxism may be old-hat in much of the world but here we're isolated, self-centered, and with the Government victimizing them—well, martyrdom —while it weeds out the faint-hearted—always invigorates a faith. As for our handful of tough dogmatists, happily they're now in exile." Ben's grin widened. "And all as ruddy well bourgeois as we!"

Instinctively I looked about—so indiscreet a conversation —but there were no trees or bushes near. I should have known that none of them would be thus relaxed unless safe from any possibility of bugging. We lapsed into silence. I'd been fascinated by the conversation, yet, listening, I felt it was words spoken in a dream . . . The night, with its grand sky, absorbed us in the universe and made of us and our concerns on this small patch of earth a mere particle.

After a while, "At least," said Shula, her voice wistful, "it's a comfort to know that Kobie, wherever he may be, is under this same sky."

"You're really convinced he's still in this country?" asked Jill.

"Of course."

"I'm not," said Ben. "What on earth can he hope to achieve? I hope to God he *has* got out, and . . ."

Alan's quiet voice intervened. "He said he would remain. He's a man of his word."

"But he did jump bail," I said.

"For him it was more immoral to submit to our corrupt laws."

"How did such a man become a Communist?" A dyed-in-the-wool Afrikaner . . . but I meant more than that; people really cared for him and worried constantly on his behalf.

"Very similar to what happened in the Spanish Civil War," said Alan; "the poets and other young intellectuals who became Marxists . . . Kobie was at Oxford in the thirties—the time of the hunger marches, the rise of fascism . . . He came home to find Africans more than ever oppressed, and the Greyshirts rampaging; there was the Broederbond too."

The Broederbond. Father had raged about them. Pro-Nazis. Men who ruled us now.

"As for the Church Militant!" I said scornfully, "more like recumbent!" And realized my train of thought must seem obscure.

"D'you mean to say you're religious?" Jill gave me no

time to clarify nor was there any simple answer to her amused indulgent disbelief.

"Well, last Sunday being Sharpeville Day I thought I'd go to church"—I was remembering again the dim interior, the incense, the lurid crucifixion which hung suspended above the aisle, the hymns circulating thinly in the air—"It really was quite comic; we prayed for all in authority to truly administer justice"—Ben snorted—"and for all in this city. Then we prayed for Ambrose Sprong"—"Oh, Cookie, and you never told me! Who on earth?"—"Apparently he was being made a deacon in Cumberland or Northumberland. Then the vicar . . ."—why should I mind so much, after all it had been naïve to go with expectation?—"The vicar preached of 'lov', and there we sat, the congregation, smartly hatted and gloved, dreaming of . . . what? Occasionally someone nodded approvingly . . . Well, I thought, Marx had a word for it."

"Ah, but why should *you* need opium? You weren't 'the people' after all!" Ben found my story diverting.

"And the anniversary of Sharpeville?" asked Alan.

"Oh, there was no mention of Sharpeville." Remembering how, afterward, I looked up Paula's note: March 21, Bach's birthday, the St. Matthew Passion. Peter's cry of remorse. "Have mercy upon me, my bones are consumed." And: "Tis your hour now, ye dread powers of darkness."

Ben got up to offer drinks. "The followers of Chairman Mao," he said, "though God forbid they ever come to power, at least they insist that action must spring from the people."

" 'The people,' " I said. "I passed some of them on Sunday morning, servants in a vacant lot, wearing blue and white robes, stomping and chanting and swaying as they circled about their prophet . . ."

Ben interrupted. "As for our Muscovites"—his reversion to the topic clearly came from a deeper perturbation than he probably would admit; he'd taken his glasses off and his eyes gazed on us with a naked innocence—"They were great on theory. Criminally optimistic." Behind his light tone hard anger lurked. "Plotted adventures that went off at half cock and landed all the best chaps in jail!" His hand resettled the glasses on his nose. "All the same, the buggers were a lot braver than I. I'd piss myself if I had to drive about with dynamite in the boot."

"And the Third World?" I asked, though what I really wanted to know was in which category, if any, Matthew belonged. "Surely Castro is relevant."

"Yes and no." Alan took up the question. "Theoretically yes, but guerrilla action, here?" He shook his head.

"But why not? Why . . . ?" Perplexity swept me. I wanted it spelled out. "What people outside wonder is why don't all the blacks rise up and knife us?"

Patiently Ben explained. "First they welcome us, right? Then with our land-grabbing they fight us for a century, assegaais against guns, right? Inevitable defeat. Since then, non-violent struggle, continually crushed, time after time, by the facts of power, of economics, of terror—yes, terror —not the ultimate as with Hitler and Stalin, though of course the S.B. are now adept at torture—I mean a continual, massive, administrative terrorizing . . . And so, the few with guts enough to organize and protest have been lopped off, decade after decade."

Jill interposed. "What about the psychological factors, the escape mechanisms, those servants Anne saw, stomping away their frustrations . . . above all the fact that oppression and insecurity breed apathy . . . ?"

"Oh God! How you all stay sane!" I couldn't contain it.

"Sane!" Ben whipped back. "Who wants to be sane when we're all so bright and beautiful?"

Ben . . . I could have bitten my tongue off. "And Matthew Marais?" I thrust the question at Ben's consciousness.

"Matt? Ah yes, where we came in . . . Matt's a product of the late forties when students assisted the miners and the Indian passive resisters. He's a sound advocate—none of Alan's forensic sparkle—but if I were in trouble I'd find it a devil of a job to choose between them, there's something about the way he moves in a case . . ."

"He goes far beyond the legal aspects to embrace the human—nothing is too much trouble," said Alan.

"Soundness is a surer way to win than brilliance, the morons you're likely to strike on the bench these days!" said Jill.

"He's been imprisoned a couple of times," added Shula, "in the Defiance Campaign and after Sharpeville."

"In short, a goody. Well, that about wraps up the seminar," and Ben's hand on the siphon poised above my drink sent a jet of soda into the glass.

Shula went off to get fresh coffee and Alan began to question Ben about his Mini-Minor—they were considering one for Jill—when across the lawn we heard Shula: "Matt! You've come after all! How lovely!" She was hugging a lean silhouette.

He joined us to pleased exclamations and a movement of welcome. Ben gave him a brandy and, with Alan, promptly drew him into discussion of some case. He looked weary, but then it was as if he shed the load in the recreation of their company.

Shula returned and began to pour fresh coffee. "Are the twins still passionate about their nursery school?" she asked Jill . . .

The moon, orange, outsized, suddenly appeared and soon filled the garden with silver radiance. The usually aloof cat, stretched on the footrest of my chair, let me run a finger down the contour of its spine. And purred. My hand searched through its soft warm fur, adjusted to rest firmly about its shoulder blades, and went with the almost imperceptible rise and fall of its breathing. I looked up into quizzical dark eyes. Matthew stood over me, offering a cigarette. I said I didn't smoke. He lit one for himself and sat down in the empty chair beside me. He made no attempt at conversation.

Shula poured him a second cup of coffee and, as he helped himself to the sugar she proffered, "We had an awfully solemn session earlier, Matt," she said. "It would have amused you . . . what on earth set us off?" She was searching back in her memory. "Oh, one thing, Cookie, you said you feel more alive here . . ."

"Why do you think that is?" I asked. I'd spoken mindlessly, to prevent Shula from moving on to more embarrassing references, but Matthew considered the question so-brely.

"In our country"—he paused to ask, "You are South African, aren't you?"—"in our country every day—whether through massive stupidity or deliberate cruelty—love and dignity and decency are destroyed. Well, once this is recognized, once responsibility to withstand such destruction is accepted, you are on the side of life . . . Yes, you are harassed and restricted, but that in itself means you have power, which is a pretty lively force." He smiled briefly. "And," he went on, "those who survive in the ugliness and absurdities of life here," he looked around his friends with an expression of great sweetness, "we have a heritage of love from those who have sacrificed themselves, who have been hanged or who are imprisoned . . . They are a living presence, they enliven us so that we trust each other . . . we feel tenderly toward each other . . ."

What had seemed dream-like, remote, had become all at once intimate.

Chapter 7

A<small>N OLD WOMAN IN A MAUVE AND GREEN SARI CAME</small>
shyly into the anteroom where I was working. "I am
Mrs. Ramchandran," she introduced herself, and as we
shook hands I said I didn't think Matthew Marais would be
long before attending to her problem.

"No, it is not for myself I am here, it is for my son
Anand."

She said no more, and sat down to wait. Ramchandran
. . . the echo of a name, how long since, twenty years?
. . . my fingertips were delicately feeling each other, like
moth wings, as I searched . . . yet it was not something
tactile but a scent I was trying to fix . . . of silks, when
you moved into the dim interior of the shop? Silks . . .
surely not. Some incense, or herbs? I could not retrieve it,
neither in my nostrils nor in words, only knew of it, pun-
gent, foreign, so that once upon a time buying silk with my
mother entranced me . . . Ramchandran—the name
had been like a spell.

Matthew came out of his room, hurried to greet her. As
he led her toward his door he paused beside my table, his

hand rested for a moment on the court record I'd been studying. "No problems?" His manner was friendly but preoccupied. "Good." And he opened the door for her.

Since my first day on the job when he'd described in precise detail the needs and form of the survey of trials, and though I'd worked in his office when I was not with Alan or the attorney concerned in these cases, there had been no more than such brief exchanges. Now I concentrated again on the case of Dan Makhana in 1964: a doctor, on trial for his life.

"We hoped," he had told the judge, "that by sabotage against installations we would open the ears of the Minister of Justice; the Government did not listen all the very many years when we tried by other ways, by peaceful methods, to win our rights, ordinary human rights."

It must have been half an hour later when Matthew and Mrs. Ramchandran emerged. He accompanied her to the lift, came straight back and into his room. I needed a file from a cabinet there and, after knocking on the door, went in.

He was sitting at his desk, oddly hunched. I didn't realize at first, then it was too late.

When he spoke his voice sounded raw. "Anand Ramchandran—that was his mother—the police want him to incriminate a friend, a man they suspect of organizing military training outside the country. They tried most of their tortures. He held out. Even through shock treatment. They came to their ultimate . . ." He broke off, stood up, strode to the window and back. He did not look at me. "Mrs. Ramchandran would have found it hard to speak of such indecency. She brought me a note which was smuggled out, I cannot tell you how."

From his desk he handed me a rumpled piece of ruled paper. In small careful writing the note reported the date and place of arrest, gave details of interrogations, and then:

> They took turns to beat me but I would not speak. Then one of them, Sgt. Jansen, tied a plastic bag over my head. I was suffocating, my hands must have waved because when they removed it and I got my breath back and still refused to speak they were furious and said I had signalled I wanted to confess. They left me some days, then one night they came for me and strapped me down on a table. They gave me the shock treatment until I said I would talk. I told something only about myself and not serious. I don't remember what, but I'd not done anything serious. But I know I did not talk about my friend because then they forced me to lay my penis on the bench. Sgt. van Rensburg told me I would never be able to have a child. The other three laughed and said obscene things. Then two of them, van Rensburg and Jansen, came at me with a plank. In the middle a rusty nail stuck out. They pressed this nail down against my foreskin. Harder. I could feel it begin to come through. Besides, I was afraid of blood poison. I said all right I would talk.

I stared at Matthew. He shook his head, then his hand rubbed across his eyes and face. He picked up his briefcase and went out. I heard him say to the receptionist, "I'll be in court."

"Trouble with you, Anne dear," said cousin Patrick when I arrived for their dinner party that evening, "is that you mix only with liberals and leftists. Time you met people who really matter. Such as Andries Coetzee, an extremely civilized Nationalist, a philosopher." With a fond smile he added, "We've invited him especially for you. I'll draw him out, it's a chance to hear about the Bantustans."

I nodded abstractedly, my eyes on the small sculpture by Kumalo, on the picture by an obscure Spanish artist . . .

"And Henry Thomson's coming," said Sally. "He's a charmer, and brilliant, my dear. But, of course, you must remember him."

When Patrick had first introduced Sally to the family, Grandpa had thought her womanly, sweet; I'd felt betrayed —how had he failed to penetrate her triviality? Probably simple jealousy on my part.

"Sally, when you were small did you ever go to Ramchandran's silk shop?" I asked.

With an apologetic smile she left me to greet the first arrivals, the Cassadys—Patrick's stockbroker and his wife.

James appeared with an ice bucket and a tray of bottles. He welcomed me and, under Patrick's appraising eye, he mixed us the driest of martinis.

Henry Thomson held my hand lightly in his. He was laughing down at me. "You've come back!" He was still undeniably attractive. As I withdrew my hand and smiled inwardly at the recollection of Shula's "a monument of ego," he was telling me how glad he was, how he'd always thought I was far too feminine to be a serious writer . . . This was the man who had destroyed Matthew's marriage.

Andries Coetzee and his wife had arrived. While Patrick made the introductions I noticed that Coetzee touched his wife's hand . . . in affection, but also, I felt, to give reassurance. A courteous man, he looked agreeable. She was shy and plain. Patrick told me they'd recently toured the States and had us comparing opinions of New York and Washington.

Scraps of other conversation broke in: "Sweetie, I wish we could, but we'll be in Japan . . ." "Reef Consolidated? No! Steer clear . . ." "Mm, I hear he's walked out on her . . ." ". . . yes! Brought my handicap down by two . . ."

The vicar had just come, a great friend of Sally's, young yet benign, who'd preached of "lov" . . . I felt so tired . . . Ramchandran . . . Matthew . . . with relief I heard Sally tell us dinner was ready. The seating, she said gaily, was unorthodox; because I was a visitor from London she'd given me the honor of having Dr. Coetzee on my right hand. She sat between the vicar and Leslie Cassady. Patrick attended to Mrs. Coetzee, then settled me in my chair.

At the table with its crystal candlesticks the flames evoked flickering reflections from the glasses, and conversation rattled along. Mouths, when not emitting words, munched sipped swallowed—the law of perpetual motion?

(A few hours earlier, Ben had said, "Even if Matt brings a case against van Rensburg and the others for assaulting Ramchandran, he won't get anywhere.")

I drank glass after glass of water.

The maid, Ellen, was assisting James, a starched white frill framing her pert face. Patrick was explaining to the

Coetzees, "James has been with us . . . how long is it, James, since you came knocking on my back door?"

"Ten years, master!" It was a jolly ritual to initiate newcomers. There followed exclamations about the value of good training, about loyalty, with Patrick pointing out that he'd been a bachelor at the time, how it was to the credit of Sally that James had survived the marriage . . .

Sally asked Coetzee about his son, who was studying at Leyden University. I clung to each fact, and in my turn discovered he had a daughter in Pretoria, and grandchildren, finding in his replies some excuse for further questioning. I liked the warm pride with which he spoke of them, and the way in which he drew his diffident wife in. Sally, when she noticed a lull, remarked, "Dr. Coetzee, I do wish you and your wife could visit our church, it has such a beautiful atmosphere. Father Hazelton has worked wonders in bringing it to life."

"Sometimes," said Patrick, his face already anticipating his joke, "I think there's grounds for divorce, when I catch Sally starching your surplice, vicar."

The Coetzees looked faintly shocked before concluding from Father Hazelton's laughter that it was all in good fun.

My glance crossed Henry's. Unfair . . . he really shouldn't be so beguiling. I couldn't resist smiling back. The woman beyond Coetzee demanded his concentration: "Henry! Did you know, my eldest, Angela, won the cup Patrick's presented . . . ?" It was for show jumping. The mother had a decidedly horsey look.

Henry launched into a description of a recent safari.

"And there we were, the truck bounding across the Kalahari, hartebeest and wildebeest in their hundreds galloping ahead of us—my God, they're beautiful creatures those hartebeest—and there's the thrill of the uncertainty . . . will we get within range in time?"

When he had finished, Leslie Cassady, who sat on the far side of the horsey woman, spoke up. "I hear the Etosha Pan's great for game."

Etosha . . . Kobie Versfeld, rumours picked up by the press said he'd been seen there, a man who resembled him had been arrested, then released with apologies. Regularly his whereabouts made headlines. Was he in Bechuanaland? Tanzania? Right here in the city? And Matthew, did he know? They were old friends, so Shula said. Was he involved?

"Henry," I said abruptly, across the table, "didn't you and Andrew Fox win the men's doubles one year at the Country Club? I see in this evening's paper that he's been banned."

There was a fractional pause as if what I'd said was not quite in good taste.

"Yes, poor chap," Henry spoke with sympathy. "Of course, he must have been up to something . . ."

(Shula'd said, "Oh God, poor Andrew!" To be banned was like having the plague.)

I started to say, "There's no charge, he can't even . . ." but I'd mistimed, no one heard, and Henry's voice went on reasonably. "What can you expect when you oppose the Government? After all, we live in dangerous days."

I tried again. "He can't even protest, everything he says is illegal now . . ."

"But, darling," Sally intervened, "he can leave the country, get a job at some university overseas. After all, he's very talented."

". . . flexible, look at Vorster," Henry's voice rose, "the way he's let ninety days lapse."

(Ben had said: "Crafty bastard will re-enact whenever he chooses.")

"Harold Wilson," came Leslie Cassady's voice, "will always take in our Reds and Pinkos!" and he chuckled at his witticism.

My God, I thought, we really are a lot of caricatures . . .

James was at my side, refilling my glass with water. And am I not closer to you, I wondered, as I looked at him, and to Ellen, than to all these people—my own people—around the table?

The flow of conversation ran smoothly again until a girl's voice carolled from beside Henry. "Seems to me . . . no difference, actually, between . . . and an orgasm . . . that sort of thing," and Dot Cassady's head, with its tawny and silver streaks, swayed like a heavy chrysanthemum toward Henry, who was laughing gustily.

Between what?—the question drifted in and out of my mind. I drank more water, and wondered: shall I go to the Eastern Cape? Since Matthew's first mention of what was being done there, his suggestion—his request really—had nagged at me. But clearly it would be a formidable venture . . . am I frightened then?

"Dr. Coetzee," Patrick's hand touched mine in delicately assumed alliance, "won't you tell us about the dialogue between your people and the Bantu?"

"Yes, Mr. Lane, the dialogue has begun." The remark caused the others to stop talking; perhaps Patrick had alerted them too to Dr. Coetzee's special experience. The silence grew respectful. Yet to me he sounded vulnerable and perhaps, I thought, turning my attention fully on him, perhaps face to face, now, it was possible for this man and me to reach, to understand . . .

"I believe we have the answer," his voice gained conviction as he went on, "to the worldwide problem of different races living in harmony."

I asked, "How does the dialogue actually happen?"

"Anne means in everyday terms," interjected Patrick.

"Well, for example, today in the Transkei Bantustan, white civil servants—Afrikaners, most of them, mark you—are happily working under the Bantu."

An appreciative murmur ran round the table. I silently remonstrated: but your entire nonsense of apartheid is because your people say they *cannot* work with blacks. From the highly polished table two knots of wood stared owlishly at me.

As if he sensed my thoughts, Patrick's hand, lightly restraining, rested on my arm. "What do you envisage, doctor, as the eventual set-up? I know my cousin is extremely interested."

I felt Coetzee was seeing me for the first time. "Well, naturally, partition. The *only* solution . . . Look at Israel, Pakistan, Ireland too . . ."

I won't tangle, I won't tangle . . . I felt my napkin rumple in my fists. I kept telling myself, we aren't caricatures, we're *real*, and, smiling at Coetzee, I made an effort. "I met a dominee recently, a charming man. Jan du Toit, perhaps you know him?" Thus I offered the dominee on a plate. Coetzee shook his head, but I could see that Patrick appreciated my contribution. His benevolent expression unreasonably provoked me. "The dominee," I went on, "was very upset about the Government's breaking-up of African families—'It cannot be Christian,' he said."

"What folk like that do not appreciate," said Coetzee mildly, "is that you cannot make an omelette without breaking eggs." He smiled agreeably, and although I well knew if I got emotional I would weaken my case, and although Patrick's knee nudged mine in warning, I persisted.

"Partition, then, Dr. Coetzee," my voice was regrettably strident, "that would mean unscrambling an omelette, wouldn't it?"

But Coetzee had been distracted by the horsey woman, who, with her face close to his, was confiding in him. "You know, doctor, our boy, he's been so cheeky lately, I really believe he's become one of those agitators." And she helped herself to soufflé from a dish proffered by James's black hands in their white gloves.

Coetzee, helping himself in turn to the soufflé, sympathized—black nationalism, yes indeed, a grievous danger.

I gulped water and announced: "Some of my best friends are African nationalists. I assure you they're not the least bit racialist."

In Sally's eyes, a phantom, and Patrick . . . so he was not intact! But Coetzee surveyed me with indulgence.

"Those are the old-fashioned types," he said, "I assure you." Very softly he continued. "However, if Bantu rule should ever be forced on my country, my people would never submit. *Never!* Our revolt, our underground, would be such as the world has not yet seen. Yes. We would be far more devilish than the Bantu could ever be. That I assure you, Miss . . ."

"Dawson," Patrick offered it. "Anne comes from London," he reminded.

"Ah, of course. You know, Miss Dawson, you liberals ought to worry about us Afrikaners. *We* are the ones faced with the black danger and UNO."

"Yes, what about that, Miss Dawson?"

A buzz of voices . . .

"Blacks in UNO can't run their own . . ."

". . . our stability here!"

"Ruin this country, then they'll be satisfied . . ."

". . . liberals!"

"Criminal . . ."

". . . Bantu . . ."

"Shut up!" All of a sudden I was shouting, bawling at them. "The lot of you! Shut up! You make me sick! In America, here, we won't be satisfied till we've driven blacks to murder, chaos! The torture! . . . this man, he's an Indian . . . I can't tell you . . . the families . . . You're the voters! Lot of bloody ostriches!"

I got up, I wanted to bang their heads together. "Business,

all you think about! It's your fault! All your fault . . .
your fault . . ." I stormed out and away . . .

The next morning—it was a Saturday and Shula was out,
taking the children to their art class—I went into the garden. No tamarisk in bloom now, nor hibiscus, but the first
dark-petalled poinsettias signalled the approach of winter. I
climbed to the corner of the kopje where unkempt grass re-
claimed the earth and shrubs grew wild. My footfalls sent
grasshoppers leaping. I found a soft patch of grass sheltered
from the cool wind and lay there, growing drowsy with the
pleasure of the sun and the grasshopper and bird sounds, the
pollen in the air . . . Numbness abated . . . if only Roger
could have heard me tangle! Roger . . . now I saw that
failure for what it was, not so much a failure in our relationship, but in myself . . . to do with living, with losing . . .
I'd used him, he'd given me a centre, a reason and object
. . . All the same, there'd been a small slice of life we'd
shared.

I stretched out a hand to tug a green stalk from its sheath
and chewed the sap from it. Strange, this aliveness, this could
be the land of the living. As for hope . . . I had hoped.
Crazy, but I had, just a bit . . . Hope, fatal here. Salutary
to be rendered hopeless by Coetzee. To live without hope,
that is to be alive . . .

After a while I went down to the house, to the telephone.
There was no reply from Matthew's chambers. I tried his
home. The African woman who answered said, "No, Mma,
Mr. Marais is not here. This morning early he was called
away."

Shula's car sounded coming up the steep drive. I hastened to meet her, to tell her all about the disaster.

"Bloody ostriches, I called them!" I could hardly believe it.

"Oh, Cookie, good for you!"

"Wish I'd thought of saying what a squalid sight, all their bottoms sticking up into the air. Except, it was not strictly true, they were glued to their chairs."

We both got the giggles. I felt a muddle of shame and pride—Lord, I must have upset Patrick and Sally who'd been so endlessly kind. "If only I'd been more coherent!" I wailed. "And my God, fancy hoping Coetzee and I might connect! As for Henry Thomson!"

"I always feel, Cookie, if you try so hard to keep a foot in two worlds you'll get the worst of both," said Shula sensibly, and not for the first time. "Anyway, life's too short. Right?"

"Right." Life is too short. All the same I would order flowers to be sent to Sally. I hadn't the nerve to telephone.

"By the way, Shula," I remarked, trying to sound casual, "I've decided to go down to the Eastern Cape . . ."

"Oh, Anne, that's marvellous."

"I tried to phone Matthew to tell him but he was out."

"He telephoned you at breakfast time—he wouldn't let me wake you—he'd just had an urgent call from Port Elizabeth to take on a case there. He had to leave at once. He said he hoped you would go down."

Part Two

Chapter 8

*F*ASTENING MY SEAT BELT I THOUGHT OF BEN'S PARTING
quip: "It's like another planet, you'll be something of a
pioneer."

The Eastern Cape . . . Grandpa's forebears had been
among the pioneers . . . settlers from Britain, refugees
really from failed crops—or was there a depression after the
Napoleonic wars—who had sailed from one end of the At-
lantic to the other, and on into the Indian Ocean, to land
on wild southern beaches—how ever did the women manage in their crinolines?—then forged their way into what
they believed was empty territory to hew a life out of the
tough brushland . . . little knowing that His Excellency
the Governor, from hundreds of miles away in Cape Town,
had decided that a human barrier would be the cheapest
form of protection against the black inhabitants. In time
the blacks were subdued by guns, by the Bible, by education.

Seven hundred and fifty miles by direct flight southeast-
ward to Port Elizabeth.

I recalled the sparkle in Ben's eye as he'd remarked,

"Should be fascinating. The most militant area, a proud record until those bastards in the S.B. decided to get their revenge."

"Revenge? For what?"

"The roots lie in history. Impress that on the great British public, they had a hand, after all. A century back, Africans had the vote, but as education spread, door after door was slammed in their faces."

"Yes, but . . ."

"Then came the defiance campaign—1952—remember?" (I, remember? A teen-ager, with Johnnie Johnston the centre of my world?) "Well, thousands defied the colour bar, the pass laws, and crowded jails, singing, laughing, particularly splendid they were in the Eastern Cape."

"But Ben, *revenge?*"

"That's what I'm telling you—fair drove the S.B. crazy, all that discipline and good humour! Been trying to get their revenge ever since; they failed dismally in the Treason Trial"—rubbing his hands in satisfaction—"and now, though the sabotage is well and truly crushed, their machine bashes on, bulldozing every crumb of protest. Those bastards have it all their own way."

The plane's drone should have been soothing . . . but I was on edge with excitement and apprehension. Deliberately I took a wallet from my handbag and checked through: passport, receipts for car hire booking and the beach cottage, the letter received the day before from an editor confirming that he'd like a feature article, my press card . . .

"Keep your press card always on you. You never know . . . besides, you won't get into the courts without it."

Now, as the plane approached what it amused Ben to call "another planet," quite suddenly I felt happy. And with this happiness a sort of inner simplicity, as if my mind was a clean slate on which significant things—beautiful? horrible? amusing?—could be written.

Chapter 9

Port Elizabeth on the Indian Ocean: I drove through the dock area, past the clock tower which commemorated the settlers—I must find the family name there—past Queen Victoria, whites only on the benches around her plinth—past shops, new banks—rush-hour traffic slowing me down—on by the law courts, past the African township —New Brighton, rows and rows of block houses almost concealed by the curves and contours of the road—then factories—one after another with familiar British and American trade signs—while trucks and vans crowded the road. A last view of the ocean sparkling under the wintry sun. Through marshes which became a lagoon, up a steep gradient past brickworks with cone-shaped furnaces and labour compound . . .

Into a region of tough aloe-speckled brushland, the trees sparse and stunted. I adjusted mental blinkers, shut out anxiety by narrowing concentration to a point on the map until, in an unexpectedly fertile valley, I came upon the reality of that point: a railway siding and a couple of buildings by the roadside.

A policeman stood outside one. I drew up and asked for the courthouse.

"This is it, lady."

I found myself explaining I was "press" come to report. Before I could think he'd led me inside, down a corridor dim and cold after the sunlight, to what could have been a small schoolroom, where on a low platform a man bulky in robes sat at a desk while men and women, white and black, were ranged on chairs and benches.

Press! Everything stopped. Surprise turned to palpable distaste. Out of the heavy silence someone left and came back carrying a chair, which gingerly I sat down on and stared at my notebook until voices took up the proceedings.

Where was Matthew? His case had only been running a day or two . . . Not that I wanted to be associated with him, at least not in the minds of the authorities, but I felt alien, isolated.

Two men sat at tables before the Magistrate: Counsels for the Defense and Prosecution; between them a blonde adjusted a tape recorder. Beside me, on a backless bench, huddled a group of Africans, three men and two women. From around their necks hung squares of cardboard, with 1 2 3 5 6 roughly chalked on. Number 1 wore an imitation leather jacket; the rest, the assorted garments of the poor.

Number 4 was in the box giving evidence. Next to him a man with a fresh complexion interpreted questions from English into Xhosa and the replies from Xhosa into English. The cardboard square marked 4 flapped in a draft of air and the man—he was quite young, bearded, in torn overalls—put up a hand to still it. I tried to piece together his defence.

He denied belonging to a banned organization, he denied attending tea parties to raise funds, he denied distributing leaflets. He seemed to deny everything.

Number 6, a girl in polka dots with only a cardigan against the cold, when it came to her turn, also denied a great deal but said that years ago she remembered seeing green and gold and black flags at street-corner meetings.

Tea break. I remained on my chair, not bold enough to join the movement to the doors. The six accused did not talk to each other, only sat on the bench in the middle of the meanly furnished room. What had become of Matthew? Why no message? Two men strolled outside: the Prosecutor and the Defence Counsel. Through the door I could see them chatting amicably. They mounted the steps and came into the room. Counsel for the Defence looked vaguely familiar. He broke into a little dance and began to sing "Ché Sera Sera." The Prosecutor took off his thick-lensed spectacles and joined in. "I asked my mother, what should I do? . . ."

The accused did not react.

Nor did they react when the Prosecutor, spectacles precisely adjusted on his nose, declared the maximum sentence to be warranted. The defending lawyer protested. The interpreter called on us to rise. The Magistrate withdrew.

The winter sun streamed in, its angle ever shifting.

"Rise in court!"

We rose. The Magistrate climbed back onto his platform. We sat down. He gazed over us and tapped his pencil absentmindedly against his cheek.

The interpreter said something in Xhosa.

The accused shuffled up. The recording machine crackled. The Magistrate pronounced: Guilty. All six. All counts. Five and a half years.

The young woman sobbed softly, the sound muffled by her hands. The others just stood. Then the oldest man began to cry.

The sunlight dazzled behind the Magistrate's dark bulk. The court broke up.

Outside, an African woman in a pink dress and doek waited with an elderly couple. They looked anxiously into the face of each of us as we came from the court. I did not try to look cheerful. The woman in pink ran past me. The Defence Counsel had emerged. She threw herself at him. He shook his head, said something. She began to weep. The old couple echoed her grief until uniformed policemen came from the court, the six accused between them. The woman in pink contrived to choke down her tears, but she could not speak, only kept nodding at the young bearded man and nodding, as if to say: It's all right. You'll come through. We'll be all right. And he nodded back. Then the policemen, perhaps out of sudden bold kindness, let him take her in his arms and whisper to her and kiss her, before he was urged along with the others to a prison van.

The interpreter was beside me. "Which paper are you from?" he asked.

I told him. "A London newspaper," I explained.

"You don't say."

"What's happened about the trial that was on?" I asked.

"It resumes tomorrow, lady. Ten o'clock."

I backed the hired car and swung onto the main road. I

drove slowly. I did not want to pass the van with the six prisoners.

An hour later I was back at the beach cottage I'd rented. I tramped restlessly from kitchen to living room to bed-room, my mind on the accused men and women, bunched together with those cardboard numbers around their necks. Number 4 had to keep holding down the card when it flapped. Number 4 . . . his wife in pink . . . I rearranged the books I'd brought. "Ché Sera Sera" rang in my brain. I thought about lunch, cut bread and cheese. The Defence lawyer in that little dance, that duet . . . I thrust the food aside. I seized a broom and strode to the outside lavatory which stood, stark white, to one side of the cottage. I swept it out with brusque strokes. Swept twice more in the cor-ners. Opened the door wide for a last hard sweep of the grit, out into the sandy path. I came back with disinfectant and scrubbing brush and had a go at the round wooden seat with its handled lid.

Then quickly I pulled on my bathing suit, ran along the clifftop road, clambered down over rocks to a small beach, and ran into the water, into shock! An extremity of cold, a clarity of blue. I swam and lay, face downward, in the salt sea, until straining lungs forced me over, and I floated, breathing deep and gazing at nothing but sky.

Back at the cottage it was almost dark when a car's head-lights swept the track and heath outside. Disturbed, hopeful, I opened the door and went out into the cold.

The car braked and a voice shouted: "Hey! I've found you at last!" Matthew's voice.

I ran to welcome him, but felt constrained as we shook hands.

"I'd no way of getting a message to you," he said. "My case was adjourned. I had to go to Pondoland."

"Pondoland!"

Inside, it was cozy from the small heater, the curtains drawn against the night. I asked him to pour some wine for us both and he explained that he'd spent two days trying to track down a witness.

"Any luck?"

"I found him all right. Darius Fortune, his name is. He's vital to our defence. For the moment he's agreed, but God knows . . ." His thumb tapped against his glass.

"But what?"

"Hm? Oh well, it wouldn't surprise me if he backs out. Can't blame him."

"You must be starving. As a matter of fact, so am I." And while I boiled potatoes and grilled steak I told about the day, the compulsive driving out of the devils. I liked to see him laugh.

"You *are* funny," he said. And, "It's good you've come, I'm glad." He stood and faced me. "You have some idea now of what's going on." He paced the kitchen.

"The woman I told you about—Number Four's wife—why couldn't she be there, in court?"

"The trials are held *in camera* in these remote villages because the State claims the courts would otherwise be mobbed, and that State witnesses would be threatened by the families and friends of the accused. You can imagine the

97

blow to the morale—at last brought from their cells to face trial and not a friendly face."

I asked why the Magistrate and police had been surprised to see me and he explained that the press hardly ever attended. "But from tomorrow, I'm told, local newspapers will cover my trial."

"What is your case about?"

"The sale of a motor van . . ."

"You can't be serious. You mean you've flown all this way?"

He nodded.

"But is it suitable for my article? What sort of person are you defending?"

"Suitable? I'm defending a schoolteacher, accused of contravening the Suppression of Communism Act." His expression was ironic. "In other words, of being a member of the banned African National Congress."

"How does the van come in?"

"The State case is that the accused sold the van to raise funds for the A.N.C."

"How can I write about that?" I laughed.

"That is your problem. I wouldn't want to influence you."

"Ben made it sound so dramatic! And you said . . ."

"I said something peculiarly atrocious is being done here. I cannot think of a better way to express it."

I felt put in my place. "Dinner's ready," I said. "Toss the salad, would you?"

Before he did so, he dipped a lettuce leaf into the dressing and tasted it. "Mm . . . You must tell the secret to Mary, my housekeeper."

We sat down at the kitchen table. The dark blue cloth, the heavy blue and white striped plates, the food and the rough wine, everything was ordinary, normal, decent . . . I thought: I like being with this man. We heard an owl hoot and smiled at each other.

"I like it here," he said.

"Please go on about your case. I promise not to be influenced! I mean, they must have been up to something . . . sabotage?" And remembered the evidence I'd listened to about tea parties to raise funds.

"Violence goes before the Supreme Court."

"Well, what are these cases about, what *was* the African Congress up to?"

"After Sharpeville African political parties were outlawed and driven underground. A small group branched off under Mandela and Makhana to organize sabotage . . . their activity, and the sabotage of the white students, came to an end with the arrests and trials of '63/'64. But the main body, most of them ordinary men and women, tried from underground to keep up protest and to raise funds to defend those who were arrested. The S.B. know they've been up to something, so they round up suspects by the hundred, lock them up, and start their interrogations . . . There they all are in the cells, eyeing each other, wondering who will cave in, who will turn up in the witness box to give evidence for the State. In the eyes of the S.B. those who hold out are guilty. If evidence needs embroidering, concocting now and then, if a witness needs schooling, why not? The accused are guilty! The State must be defended!"

We took our coffee through to the sitting room.

"Who are these State witnesses?" I asked.

He lit a cigarette and found himself an ash tray; then: "Informers—old hands at the game. Neighbours with a grudge. Prisoners—who knows whether they might not improve their condition? Above all, those who know that if they'd not agreed to go into the witness box, they themselves would be in the dock. And they all say they've come only to tell the truth!" His laugh was bitter. "The Government asserts you can't make an omelette without breaking eggs. That should be the national motto rather than 'unity is strength.'"

He paused, thought for a moment, stubbed out his cigarette and went on grimly. "There Anne, that's what you have to convey . . . precisely what 'breaking eggs' means, what it does to the lives of men and women. You're a writer . . . there's your problem. How to describe the petty monotonous trials in these tinpot courts, with mediocre third-rate villains and unsensational heroes, and at the same time bring to life the drama . . . the deliberate attempt to destroy the self-respect of a community."

"And the 'hero' you're defending, who is he?"

"Not a 'hero,'" he smiled. "A 'heroine.' Her name is Beatrice Qaba. She's been in jail awaiting trial for seventeen months."

A prison van drew up outside the courtroom. From the front jumped a thickset short African, wearing dark glasses.

His hair shone, and had a neatly ploughed parting. He unlocked the gate of the wire cage. "Maak gou!" he commanded the invisible occupant. A woman emerged, middle-
aged, in a green beret and long gray coat.

Matthew met her in the doorway, tall and angular beside
her comfortable shape. He took her hand, spoke quietly to
her. His calm reassurance and warmth elated me. Beatrice
Qaba's plain soft face appeared tired but her eyes were alert.
After seventeen months in a prison cell, what did the world
look like? She went inside with Matthew and through the
open doorway I could see them as they sat together on a
bench in consultation.

On a rock in the yard outside, I sunned myself. I could
hear trains shunting back and forth at the railway siding
which served the surrounding plantations. A big American car drove up. Four men got out. One, in his fifties, nar-
row-shouldered, neat but for a drooping moustache, went
into the small room next to the court. The Magistrate . . .
what did it feel like to be a power in this backwoods place?
A young man, sober-faced, with thick curly hair close-
cropped at the sides and back, giving a coxcomb effect, adjusted the white-tabbed collar of his Prosecutor's robes and
headed for the outside lavatory. The others were obviously
Special Branch. Did they really travel, all together, twice a
day, the thirty-two miles? What on earth did they talk
about? Could it always be of rugby or gardening?

One of the S.B. approached me. He was not bad looking,
only his blue eyes were too stony for comfort. He moved
with a heaving of weight from side to side of his powerful
body and looked me over as he passed . . . My hand held

a stick, scratched doodles in the ground . . . "Wait for me Mr. Lubbe!" and the other S.B., thin-necked, bald, smiling, hurried after the big man. As he caught up, I heard his tittering remark, "I see the traitor Afrikaner's inside with the prisoner." Then, as they reached the door to the courtroom, almost in the same breath, "Gooie môre, meneer Marais," he called cheerfully.

"Morning, Sergeant Smit," Matthew's low voice sounded.

When I went inside, the big man Lubbe was saying loudly to a pot-hatted matron and a keen-looking youth, "I must have your press cards." I joined them and produced mine as well. He studied each with surly disgust, pausing longer over mine with its foreign connotation.

"Rise in court!"

As the Magistrate seated himself he glanced gloomily at the three of us ranged on a bench at the back and adjured "the press" not to mention the name of any State witness.

Matthew, alongside the tape-recordist and the Prosecutor, sat half turned toward Beatrice Qaba, whose chair was a few paces behind his.

The Prosecutor rose. "I call Witness Jolobe."

A well-dressed, self-confident man entered the witness box. In a bold voice he declined the services of the interpreter.

"Now, Jolobe," the Prosecutor led, "will you tell His Worship about your position early in 1961?"

"I was secretary of a branch of the African National Congress. It was March 1961 that we held a meeting, Darius Fortune, Handyman Mani . . ." and he rattled off several names.

"A legal meeting?"

"Illegal."

He gave minute details about the meeting held more than four years earlier—the time, the place, and who said what— he must have a phenomenal memory.

"Then what happened?"

"Your Worship, we were talking about how to raise funds when into the meeting came a woman."

"Who was this woman?"

"The accused. And Darius said, 'This is comrade Beatrice Qaba, she will speak to us.'"

"Yes. Then?"

"Then she said, 'The A.N.C. has a new plan. We must use violence to achieve our freedom. It is the only way!'"

Matthew was up. "Your Worship!" The Prosecutor sat down. The court was quiet. Beatrice stirred. Jolobe stared out of the window.

"Yes, er, Mr. Marais?" said the Magistrate.

"I submit that this evidence is irrelevant. No allegation is made in the indictment about violence. Is my learned friend introducing a new case against the accused?"

The Prosecutor was up, assuring the court that he was about to establish relevance.

"What did the accused say?" he asked Jolobe.

"She said we must raise funds to buy explosives and weapons. She sold a van for this."

Matthew was again on his feet.

"Mr. Marais," the Magistrate's voice was glum, "I appreciate your zeal on behalf of your client, but I am satisfied

the evidence is of so serious a character that it should be allowed."

Matthew glanced back at Beatrice and reluctantly sat
down. She was writing earnestly in a notebook. The black
S.B. was watching her, his face relaxed. I realized now who
he must be. Sergeant Mfaxa, of course, who'd been known,
so Ben had said, to stride into a barber shop in the township
and stand there looking round in a gesture of bullying vanity—I could picture him, thick legs planted firm, his feet
were incongruously small in highly polished black shoes—
"I am Sergeant Mfaxa!" he had taunted his fellow Africans,
"and I can put any one of you—any one!—in jail, if I
choose!"

Beatrice Qaba glanced up suddenly, conscious of his gaze.
She looked him full in the face, her stare flat. His gaze hardened . . . Ben had said someone had tried to kill him, but
an African leader, a Communist, ordered "no acts of terror."

There was a loud din of train shunting, of clanking un-
coupling of trucks, and Jolobe's evidence became inaudible.

"Adjourn for tea!" announced the Magistrate, and stalked
out.

Matthew turned his chair to join Beatrice in consultation.
I accompanied the other journalists and found that next to
the court was a store—a shed lined to the ceiling with
shelves stacked with bright cottons, blankets, underwear,
and hats, while on the floor stood sacks of corn and potatoes
and oranges and behind the counter cigarettes, popcorn,
chewing gum, toothpaste, ink, pens, and little liver pills were
displayed—everything that a farmer disinclined to drive into

town, or a farm labourer unable to drive into town, might require. One corner with a half-dozen tables formed a café where we had tea. My companions told me they represented local newspapers and I questioned them about the surrounding valley.

"Full of English types," said the young man, "prosperous."

"There's a Women's Institute," the pot-hatted woman added.

"I suppose they couldn't care less about what's going on in this ghastly little courtroom," I said, and wondered if I'd been incautious, but the young man's smile seemed to be one of collusion.

Outside again it was warmer in the sunlight. Voices made me look up. From a window over the court protruded a woman's head crammed with curlers under a mauve net which framed her flushed face. She gossiped raucously with someone inside. Above the window was a sign: MARCEL HAIRDRESSING SALON. A black woman appeared at the adjacent window and shook out a duster.

I went on to the courtroom, eager to find out from Matthew what the new evidence signified, but he and Beatrice were still talking gravely together.

The court was reassembling. Now the Prosecutor must surely come to the point.

He was up. "Jolobe, the van which the accused sold . . ." he began, and launched into prolonged questioning about its make, the purchaser, the price. Not a word about the explosives, the guns . . . only a monotony of detail . . . enough to stun . . .

Finally: "Adjourn for lunch!"

Matthew hurried out. Beatrice Qaba took a package from her pocket and opened it—it contained sandwiches. Lubbe was watching. He gave an order to a policeman who hurried to her. "Not in here," he said, not unkindly. "Back in the van." She closed the package, went out, and clambered slowly into the cage. The policeman locked its gate. She sat, and as I passed she smiled at me and I was grateful.

In the store I could see Matthew using the telephone only a yard or two from a table at which the Magistrate, the Prosecutor, Lubbe, and Smit were settling down. He quickly concluded his call and joined me at the table farthest from theirs.

At once I put it to him: "You said last night that violence goes to a higher court, but Jolobe says she was raising funds for arms . . ."

"I was referring to acts of violence. Jolobe has done no more than allege talk."

"But what's the point then . . . ?"

"Exactly what was achieved. To create an atmosphere of violence. At first, sentences in these trials were limited to a year or two; then, suddenly, two things happened. Instead of people being charged simply with membership, the charge was broken down into four or five counts—membership, furthering the aims, collecting funds, distributing leaflets, and so on. Each count with a maximum of three years. The other development was that allegations of violence were made—never acts, only talk—and at once sentences became more severe. As a result there have been sentences of up to ten years. Gratifying for the S.B."

I looked at Lubbe and the Magistrate, the Prosecutor and Smit, eating their stew. The Magistrate's voice rose: ". . . a hundred and forty for three!"

"Is there cricket?" I asked Matthew. "But how, it's winter? Oh yes, in England." Then I saw his face. I touched his sleeve. "I'm sorry to rattle on." He shook his head and smiled. "You're worried?" I said.

"That telephone call came from an attorney. The headmaster of the school where Beatrice taught refuses to speak for her character. I suppose it could cost him his job." The defence, he went on to explain, was dependent on Darius, who had owned the van, had lived with Beatrice, and when he'd gone to Pondoland had had her sell it for him.

He pushed his plate aside. He'd hardly eaten. As we came out of the store he went ahead and called a policeman, asked that Beatrice Qaba be fetched from the van. She emerged to join him, he bent toward her and said something that made her laugh. They went, laughing together, into the court.

Not far from where I waited in the sun stood Sergeant Smit, peaceably smoking. A small car drove up. A woman got out, elegant in tweed. From the back seat she lifted a heavy sack, then glanced around and swiftly approached him. "Are you Sergeant Smit?" She had one of those voices that assume everyone else is a Tory too. She thrust the sack into his arms. "Kindly see that Miss Qaba gets this food. I have spoken to your C.O. Some of us in the valley will supplement the awful prison diet with oranges and meat. Every day!"

So I'd been wrong. The valley was not wholly indifferent . . . I must tell Matthew.

Court reassembled.

Matthew rose to cross-examine. His red hair dishevelled, his face pale, he leafed idly through his notes. Casually he asked, "When were you arrested, Jolobe?"

"Must have been June, in 1963."

"When released?"

"July sometime. It was about two weeks."

"Why were you not charged?"

"I do not know."

"Were you surprised?"

"No."

"Why not? After all, Jolobe, you'd been an important official of an illegal organization?"

"No, nothing surprises me."

For all the casualness of Matthew's questioning, the relaxed arrogance of Jolobe's replies, and the hostile nature of their roles, a bond linked these two men, a tension . . .

"Why are you giving evidence against the accused?"

"There is no reason."

"No reason?"

"I told the truth." Jolobe's voice reverberated. "I am only telling the truth. I don't class myself as a traitor. If I am, so should Nelson Mandela be. And Makhana!"

"Mandela was no informer. Makhana disclosed no names." Matthew's voice was stern. "You know that perfectly well, Jolobe. Such men spoke only of their own actions."

The Prosecutor was protesting.

"Mr. Marais!" The Magistrate. "Must I remind you . . ."

Matthew gave the merest bow. He paused, then, "Incidentally, Jolobe, against how many people have you given evidence?"

"Well, it is hard to say . . ."

"Try, Jolobe . . . would you say five? . . . twelve?"

Jolobe appeared to do some mental arithmetic, and looked pleased. "Well, Your Worship, I think it must be more than fifty . . . Yes, I would say fifty-eight."

"Ah. Fifty-eight men and women . . . Now, Jolobe, in your evidence you said Beatrice Qaba told a meeting to raise funds for explosives?"

"Yes."

"In March 1961?"

"Yes."

"The accused will deny your evidence about this meeting. I put it to you, Jolobe, that Beatrice Qaba could not have been there. It was an executive meeting, a secret meeting. She'd have had to force her way in."

"She did. Darius asked her."

"And this secret meeting, you say, took place in March 1961?"

"Yes."

"And I put it to you, she could not possibly have spoken of violence in *March* 1961. Mandela, Makhana, the top leaders, did not decide to switch from a policy of non-violence until the end of May 1961!"

"No, she did! Weapons, she said. And she told us we must make people obey, even if it meant violence."

"Oh, assaults now, do you mean?"

Jolobe was looking around as if the answer was in the air. Beatrice, who'd sat erect, drooped, all at once forlorn.

"Yes, weapons, explosives."

"Jolobe! Let me remind you of the evidence you gave about this same meeting in a trial eighteen months ago." Matthew with grim concentration perused a document. "Your Worship, I have here the court record. Jolobe, you gave the names of the others, the names you mentioned to-day. Not once then did you mention Beatrice Qaba!"

"I was not asked about her."

"Ah. Nor, in long cross-examination, did you once say anything about violence?"

"I was not asked . . ."

"And the new plan. Today you say this meant resorting to violence. Yet according to your previous evidence the new plan was concerned with reorganizing so that the A.N.C. could function secretly?"

"No, it was also a plan to prepare for violence."

"How was it, then . . . "

The winter sun poured in, relentless. The Magistrate asked for the green curtains to be drawn. In a court somnolent with unseasonal heat Matthew pursued the details back and forth. Surely now Jolobe must be caught out . . . His arrogance! And that fantastic memory!

"One other point, Jolobe," Matthew spoke offhandedly. "When did you last see Handyman Mani?"

"I have not seen him properly, Your Worship, just glimpsed him as I was leaving the cells." Jolobe spoke with certainty.

Three forty. The Magistrate adjourned. Beatrice thrust

her notebook into Matthew's hands. The schoolmistress was like a pupil presenting an essay to a respected teacher.

I went ahead to Matthew's car, watched Magistrate, Prosecutor, and Special Branch climb into their car. Chatting and in good humour, they drove past me. Lubbe's eyes met mine, dead on, with a chill fractional amusement . . .

Beatrice and Matthew came out, followed by Mfaxa and the police. As we drove off, from the van she waved cheerfully to us. "That woman," said Matthew, "she has guts. She knows the State will have several more witnesses lined up, that we depend on Darius, and the odds are he'll fail us . . ."

Above us as we headed for Port Elizabeth the sky began to glow, clouds flared with color. He drove fast, too fast, absorbed in thought.

Gradually I sensed an easing in his tenseness, he was driving less dangerously. "It's very rare, your propensity for silence," he remarked.

"My grandfather blamed himself for it. He thought I'd become too serious. 'You should have more fun,' he used to say. 'Look at Sally.' Which made me furious! I thought her shallow." We laughed. He slowed down to light a cigarette.

"You must meet Oliver Woolley," he said. "He's a doctor, something of a saint the way he copes with defence in all these trials . . . struggles to find lawyers, witnesses, funds, the lot!"

"Shula told me they're in touch about raising funds."

We came over the last ridge, then down past the brickworks with the compound beginning to fill with dark figures. We saw the lagoon ahead, the expanse of water a mirror for the flaming sky. We drove through the marshes, and on.

"Over on the left," he said, "that's Rooihell—North End jail."

A gray massive building. "Why *Red* Hell?"

"There's a royal coat of arms over the entrance, and the Cape accent for 'royal'—'rooihell'."

Behind which of those barred windows had Beatrice Qaba lived, these seventeen months?

As soon as court assembled the next day the rumpus began. First there was Lubbe talking to the Prosecutor, who rose and announced there had been a threat, an anonymous note shoved under the door of the police station cell, a threat to kill Jolobe! A grating of chairs, a holding themselves ready of S.B. and instructions to the police from the Magistrate: "Investigate immediately!" And we press were warned again not to divulge witnesses' names.

"Urgent investigation proceeding!" announced Lubbe.

The pot-hatted lady had drafted a suitable headline: *Red Trial—Threat to Kill in Schoolteacher Case.*

"What odds," remarked the keen young man, "that's the last we hear of the sinister threat!"

"You're learning fast," I said.

Handyman Mani was in the witness box. His narrow shaved head bobbed as he took the oath. Then he replied to the Prosecutor's opening questions. "Yes, I am a prisoner on

Robben Island . . . I am serving a sentence of two years because I attended an illegal meeting . . . The meeting was in March 1961 . . ." He lolled against the side of the box.

Questions and answers accumulated in the atmosphere. The evidence was virtually what Jolobe's had been. Eventually: "Then Darius stood," said Mani, "and he told us: 'Comrade Beatrice Qaba has come to speak.' Then she said, 'Our new plan is violence. Violence is the only way to fight oppression.' "

Matthew was up. "Your Worship, I must request that my learned friend lead his witness in proving the charges, or desist from . . ."

The Prosecutor was back on his feet but Matthew refused to give way. Tension rose. "Your Worship," Matthew's voice was firm, "in leading the evidence of a previous witness, my learned friend promised that he would show relevance . . ."

The Magistrate: "Yes, Mr. Marais, and the court is satisfied that relevance was established." He nodded to the Prosecutor to continue.

"Did the accused say anything else, Mani?"

Mani looked vague. The Prosecutor tried again. "Did she say what sort of violence?"

"She said, 'Rifles, machine guns, petrol bombs.' She told us policemen's houses must be burned. Even Sergeant Mfaxa's!"

Mfaxa's eyes were shining. Near him sat Lieutenant Lubbe. The alternating voices of the Prosecutor and Mani droned on . . . they were again concentrating on the meeting, on the van. Across the floor a shaft of sunlight wavered, then settled, irradiating countless motes which ceaselessly circulated. A gust of wind had parted the curtains. The blonde, vacant-faced, sat with one hand idle on the taperecorder. The interpreter sat dozing in a corner. I looked at Matthew, at Beatrice, at the other journalists. I had this powerful feeling that we sat in the presence of evil.

Matthew opened his cross-examination. "Mani, just remind me of your evidence-in-chief. About how, so you said, the accused came into the meeting?"

Mani's eyes rounded with concentration. "Darius said: 'This is . . .' No. He said, 'Beatrice . . .' No. I am trying to repeat it word perfect."

"In fact, Mani, that meeting with Beatrice Qaba never took place, did it?"

"No no! I am sorry. It had. It did took place. Now, just one moment . . . Darius said, 'Comrade Qaba, she will tell us about a new plan.' Is that word perfect?"

"No."

"No. I also have such an opinion . . ."

"And how do you explain," Matthew's anger was mounting, "that when you gave evidence about this alleged meeting in a trial eighteen months ago—I have here the court record—you neither mentioned Beatrice Qaba nor the discussion of violence?"

The Prosecutor was up.

"Yes," the Magistrate, "really, Mr. Marais, I must ask you to keep to one question at a time." He looked at his watch. "A suitable moment to adjourn?" he suggested.

Outside, the stylish woman in tweed waited with oranges

and meat for Beatrice. Suddenly Lubbe bore down on her. "No more food parcels!" he was almost shouting, his face red. "No newspapers either!"

Matthew, from the doorway of the court, had heard. With cold disdain he confronted Lubbe. "Mr. Lubbe, this is ridiculous. You know well that these are *rights*. You cannot . . ."

"Orders from the Commandant! I'm telling you, Mr. Marais!" Lubbe stood his ground like a furious bull. He was in his element.

Matthew stared him grimly in the face, then told him he would at once telephone the Commandant, and make a formal protest to the court.

The Commandant, said Lubbe, grinning, would be at lunch; as for the afternoon, he was due at a police parade.

The woman was stiff with disgust. Beatrice, who watched with resignation, took her package from her pocket and was locked in the cage.

When court reassembled Matthew made the protest: the accused had been deprived arbitrarily of her rights. No doubt, the Magistrate said, the Commandant would advise in the morning. Now, Counsel should please resume cross-examination.

"Mani, you and Jolobe"—something in Matthew's manner, something beyond the anger of the unpleasant incident, alerted me—"when did you last see each other?"

"We have been in a cell together." Mani, hands in pockets, was smiling contentedly.

"When was this?"

"These last three days."

"How is it, then, Jolobe said he only glimpsed you?"

The smirk faded from Mani's face, his eyes narrowed and flickered as he considered this development.

"It is . . . it is because we Bantu, you know, we are not allowed to throw—as I would say—to throw a strong glimpse, to each other because, you know, Bantu do even speak by eyes. So we are guarded, to an extent that we should not even throw strong glimpses . . . even, you know, Your Magistrate, Your Worship I mean, a person in the street when you throw a strong glimpse he will stand and stop . . ."

The foxy insolence of Mani's appearance and manner gave a sinister aspect to a performance that might otherwise have been comic.

"Mani!" the Magistrate interrupted. "Just tell the court straight now, who were you in the cell with?"

"With Jolobe, like I said . . ."

"Anyone else?"

"With a certain Mfaxa, you know, Your Magistrate, Your Worship. The one who watches us."

Matthew cut in: "Mfaxa is with you all the time?"

"All the time."

Sergeant Mfaxa looked less than his bright self.

"When he goes to relieve himself he takes you?"

Mani was silent.

"No answer?"

"No. There is an answer. There is . . . Yes, there must be an answer. Each and every question has to have its answer."

The Magistrate uttered a rumble of impatience.

Mani pricked his ears. "You can carry on, Your Worship, but I say each and every question has to have its answer."

"Mani!" Matthew's voice rang through the green-glowing stuffy courtroom. "There is a conspiracy in this case. You and Jolobe have both given evidence in previous cases about the new plan. Not once did either of you then say it meant a change to violence! Now you both alter your evidence. Just as now you both say Beatrice Qaba was present at that meeting in March 1961."

"Mr. Marais," the Magistrate, "is it necessary to remind you . . ."

Matthew was like a man running hard, but in slow motion, trying to reach something that urgently must be reached, and failing . . .

Chapter 10

MATTHEW, DUFFEL-COATED, HIS LEGS SPRAWLED, HALF sat, half leaned on a stone wall which buttressed the lofty heights to which we had driven. Behind us aloes thrust thorny flaming candelabra from the dry earth. In front the world fell away. We gazed down on the valley of the Sunday's River. Far off, beyond square after square of orange groves, we could make out the cluster of eucalyptus and poplars surrounding the railway siding and the courthouse. It was his first break from the chafing tedium of the trial.

"Over to the left," I pointed, "that's the polo field. Just beyond the siding. There's a Women's Institute too."

He laughed. "You certainly get your background filled in."

"Very relevant . . ."

He breathed deeply—the air was purer, lighter, up here. Way down below we could see a handsomely laid out farm. There was no sign of movement around the spacious veranda of the house. But in the fields black labourers were digging. A child hop-skipped along a winding track heading for the huts where women were active over pots. From several fires filaments of smoke ascended to unite and hover on the still air.

Another time, another place, and this settlement could have moved one by its simplicity . . . in Australia, for instance. But here . . . now . . .

Matthew indicated a cluster of daisies, visible beyond nearby rocks. "They remind me of a poem . . .

> Ons hoer nog verdwaasd
> Klein blou Namakwaland-madeliefie,
> Iets antwoord, iets glo, iets weet . . .*

"A girl wrote that, Ingrid Jonker . . . Do you understand Afrikaans?"

"More or less. When you speak, it's not like the guttural stuff of my jingoistic schoolgirl memories."

"But it's a poetic language!" With his protest his accent became more pronounced, his hand brushed through his hair in exasperation. "And listen—'motrëen'—that soft soft rain. And 'douvoordag'—dew before day—before daybreak, that means." He laughed. "You see!" He was all gaiety. "Scratch me and you find ''n ware Afrikaner.'"

A real Afrikaner. But I preferred to apply its other meaning: a true Afrikaner, yes, that precisely described him. He was watching me, he too had become reflective. I noticed the faint freckles across his nose and brow. His eyes did not waver. I looked at his hands, resting on the wall. Beside them lay a loose stone, small, oval, shiny-smooth. He'd seen it too. He picked it up, it lay in the palm of his hand—

* Still dazed, we hear a small blue Namaqualand daisy answer, believe, and know.

almost black with complex markings. His fingers closed over it, approving what they felt. He gave it to me. It was still warm from his touch. Our silence held, and again we considered the valley below.

Great-grandfather's country. We leaned against old stones, stones that were here when he and his kind had passed this way . . . I felt pride at the luxuriance they'd wrought out of the unknown wilderness, often with little but their bare hands and resolution. Resolution, which was what Beatrice Qaba showed day after day . . . Now there was a different sort of unknown to venture into, different things to discover, a different form of settling . . .

I shivered suddenly. "Mfaxa!" I said loudly, and then saw the funny side of it. "He reminds me of an Afrikaans poem at school," I went on.

> "Nader kruip die Zulumag,
> kruip swart adders om die laer." *

"No wonder you had no feeling for the language!" Then Matthew's smile faded. "Think what my people would be if they were not in Africa. Harmless, amiable . . . a few cranks, of course, but they could work off their bigotry within their own community, like villagers in one of those Continental films. You know, Piet Retief had fine ideas a century ago . . . after all, the Boers were the first tribe in Africa to fight for freedom. Ach, but look at them to-day!"

* Nearer crept the Zulu horde, crept black adders around the laager.

On the way back to the car, "I'm glad you're an Afrikaner," I told him.

He looked surprised. "That's a rare compliment in today's world!" Which made us both laugh.

"I suppose you symbolize something for me, out of my childhood . . ."

"So long as you're glad . . ."

I asked about the rest of Ingrid Jonker's poem. "It tells," he said, "about our divided house. About the heart closed against itself, the wire fences, camps, and locations, which separate us. Yet, she says, beyond all that, beyond the silence, beyond our torn land . . . dazed though we are, we hear a small blue Namaqualand daisy answer, believe, know . . ."

We had reached the car, and as we drove down from the heights to the spacious, fruitful valley below, "Have you thought," he asked, "what this country could become? The land . . . and the wealth; above all, the people, the splendid people!" Then he told me about the days of hopefulness, when he'd been a student . . . people of all races and beliefs claiming rights and freedoms . . . how they'd called on Smuts, just back from drafting the charter of the United Nations, to abolish the pass laws. And later—"Why, it was only six years ago!"—how Lutuli toured the country, addressing huge meetings, packed with whites, blacks, Indians, coloured people and—" 'Somlandela Lutuli,' that's what we'd sing—we will follow Lutuli . . ." And even when all this was outlawed, when thousands were imprisoned or restricted, there was still the comradeship. "But today, we are diminished . . . we are scattered . . . Yet hope, though it is denied, will never be destroyed . . ."

North End jail, alias Royal, alias Rooihell, on a Saturday afternoon. I waited in Matthew's car outside the women's section which looked onto a cemetery and a stretch of beach where sewers evacuated.

A white woman emerged from the main door; hard-chested in khaki, a wardress; unyielding in her stride she went along the gravel path which divided neat lawns. Inside the jail a black woman was cleaning a window. She stopped and, shadowy face through shadowy glass, stared out toward the road with its unceasing traffic.

Matthew appeared at the main door, briefcase in hand. As he moved quickly down the steps toward me, I thought: I love him. Matthew, I love you!

Love and longing shouted inside me. I lowered my eyes, controlled my voice, and, "How was she?" I asked.

"Just splendid! I've been frank. She knows that if Darius lets us down our last hope is to undermine their evidence about violence, which means bringing Dan Makhana from Robben Island, and Oliver Woolley estimates that will cost hundreds."

His hand turned the key in the dashboard, pulled out the starter, prepared to let the brake off . . . each gesture, just as each syllable he'd uttered, pierced my awareness. Slowly we were driving off when we heard voices shouting orders, saw guards loading black prisoners into a cage-topped van outside the men's jail. Their movements were grotesque. I was baffled, then, "Matthew, look!" I almost screeched. Two of them had become entangled and as they thrust, shoved, cursed, we could see that it was not, as in a three-legged race, one man's left leg shackled to the other's right; each man was trapped by his left leg to the next man's left leg.

Twenty-four—no, twenty-six of them . . .

"They're being sent to the Island," Matthew's voice was low. "I'd heard they were chained . . . but not that it was like this. They've got four hundred miles to go."

All the way to my cottage I gazed out of the window at the sea, my feelings in turmoil, and was relieved at the discipline of activity when, on arrival there, I faced my typewriter, wound paper in, and started to type—he'd asked if I would mind taking down a letter, a complaint to the Commissioner of Prisons.

Afterward, in my patch of a garden we watched a yellow bird gruesomely eat what appeared to be the only grasshopper.

"A bokmakierie," he said. "That's the call it gives." And he showed how to tie a marrow bone to a nearby aloe. Whatever we did, whatever we watched, had acquired an element of rapture that was agonizing so long as I had to pretend casualness—Shula's words, "He's shut out women . . . he withdrew absolutely," waved like a warning banner above my head.

While we waited, expectant, "Anne," he said, "you are patient with me, I can't think why you bother."

"No bother . . ."

"When you first came along," the thought seemed to amuse him, "I took Alan's word that you'd be useful, but my goodness, I thought, who's this cool young woman, clearly distrustful?"

"You mean you noticed?" The trivial recollection made my heart leap.

"Noticed!"

"Well, you were somewhat alarming—interested only in my usefulness! Then what you said about my article on the pass laws—I felt so happy." I dared to look up into his face. A shutter had come down. I dreaded what next I might precipitate but persevered, determined to reach him. "That night, was it just chance that you came, after all, to the Lowens'?"

He was pointing, the bird was pecking at the marrow bone. It flew to the topmost tuft of aloe. "Bokmakierie!" Well, more or less, Matthew's grin conceded . . .

"Chance? No. It struck me, while we sheltered from the rain, how beautiful you were. I wanted to look at you again, to make sure."

His voice was so flat, his manner so matter-of-fact in uttering the stunning words that I felt as if I clutched at empty air. And when he looked immediately at his watch, said, "Come on, you promised me a walk," I hurried to accompany him and again found relief in action as we set off through the heath which quilted the clifftops. Below, waves lapped against the rocks. I chose a safe subject which had the added advantage of having become for me the most romantic in the world, and asked about his family.

"Not much to tell. My father was a farmer, very upright, stern I suppose. Patriotic! He had a bust of Oom Paul Kruger in the hall. My mother? She had a capacity for happiness." He was watching a gull swoop low over the heath and rise in a great arc toward the sea which stretched like glass to the horizon; his face for a while remained brilliantly happy. "And there was Tante Annetjie, my father's sister. I loved her. She was the first rebel of the family. When she was twenty she went to visit relatives in Holland and eloped to Venice with a painter. A big woman, generous . . . when we get back to Johannesburg I'll show you a picture."

We could see a fisherman nimbly crossing rocks wet from the tide's withdrawal.

"Tell me about your house."

He laughed. "Nothing to it, what matters is Shem and Mary, who look after me, you'll like them." Crazy, but my hopes soared.

Ahead of us a young coloured man, in white shoes, ambled with his girl, his arm about her shoulders, intensifying in me the longing to be held, to hold . . .

"Barren, I suppose the house is . . . I'm hardly there . . ." He seemed to struggle with some thought, to be about to express it, then, brusquely, he declared, "The fact is, there's no time for personal things."

With extreme caution I ventured to tease, "At what point does that become an escape?"

"An escape!" His indignation was disproportionate. "Psychological labels! You've seen what's going on!"

"You choose to misunderstand me!"

"Choose?"

"Involvement! What's the use unless it's personal too!" Anguish, anger, terror—I no longer knew what I felt.

"What are you trying to say?"

"Ach, it's hopeless. Forget it."

He shrugged and said nothing more. We strode on. We were approaching the cottage, then, "I was unfair," he said simply.

"I'm sorry," I said; I felt utterly deflated. "Come and have a drink."

"To end hostilities?" He made a joke of it. That he should dare to sound cheerful!

"You'll be at the Woolleys' party?" I asked. He thought not, he had to give an opinion in a local case and study briefs from Johannesburg. A dark wave of moodiness threatened to engulf me.

He was finishing his brandy when he remarked, "Sergeant Smit drinks a bottle of this stuff a day."

"How on earth do you know?"

"Bumped into him in the hotel. He was pretty far gone. Told me it's the only way he tolerates his job. A decent fellow really, I suppose not bright enough for other jobs, and now he's trapped."

(Smit, who'd mocked Marais the traitor.)

Putting his glass down, he got up to go.

"Listen!" I said disagreeably. "I've no time for Smit. You're so bloody forgiving."

"Not always," he said, his voice cold.

Would he never get over that woman? Ashamed and miserable at my irretrievable ugly words, yet I had to retaliate, to punish. "It's hopeless, all our activity!" I said sarcastic, accusing. "We must be out of our minds! Like the spider I found in the bath this morning which had spent the night weaving a web! Useless."

"Annie, no!" His hand was firm on my arm in reproach. "The campaign will be won how ever many fall by the way. We're none of us indispensable but we have to go on. My dear, you must believe this."

When you say it, how beautiful "Annie" sounds . . . but already he'd driven away.

The Woolleys' party, though small, was a success . . . sometimes things were just so damn funny. Now we were laughing because Walt Tree had turned up from Washington to do a series on apartheid for some magazine . . . he'd already visited two courts, next he intended to cover the Qaba trial.

The thought kindled Oliver Woolley, a bearded, infinitely kind man with an aggressive manner. "Can't you see them, dear Anne? Lubbe, the Magistrate, and that little twerp of a Prosecutor, when they discover their fame has spread to the New World!"

Yes, I found the thought of their collective crossness wildly amusing . . . my laughter helped to keep at bay the longing for Matthew that continually invaded me . . . Had I irrevocably broken our friendship? Could I tolerate the strain of mere friendship?

Oliver pounced again. "Did you hear tell of that religious magistrate?" And he adopted a pious expression, spoke with a Cape accent: "This court finds you guilty. It sentences you to four years' imprisonment. It sentences you with a prayer in its heart. The court hopes you will meditate during these four years and reform your ways."

It was so awful it was hilarious.

Adelaide Woolley spoke up: "And that prosecutor, remember, Ollie darling?" She turned to the rest of us. "He got a man sentenced to five years—he'd been ruthless in his cross-examination and had called for a stiff sentence, then afterward he goes to see the poor fellow in his cell and says, 'Please, Elias, I want you to understand I couldn't help it. It's my job, you see.'"

If you laughed this much you solved your problem of not knowing whether to laugh or cry because in the end you were doing both anyway.

"Each of us whites involved in these trials," Oliver spoke with an acid gravity, "masturbating away like mad!"

There was a tremor of shock. Then: "Oliver, you *are* idiotic!"

"Honestly, how can you say that of the defence?"

"Yes, the defence too! We're all part of the same evil game!"

"What Ollie means . . ." Adelaide tried to placate, "the first time he'd been in court, he came home and said, 'Jesus! how does one live through this?'"

I was furious. "Our corruption, what does *that* matter!"

"Of course it matters!"

"No! Nothing is more awful than Beatrice Qaba's suffering," I insisted.

"I guess the imagining could be worse than the experience?" Walt asked Oliver.

"No, man, please, that is *not* what I was saying!" Oliver

protested, and with me he reasoned: "If only you could see. Surely you see, Anne, whatever they suffer, they're the only ones who keep some integrity."

What would Matthew think . . . that it was egocentric moralizing? Matthew . . .

"Talking of integrity, do you know about Kobie Versfeld?" someone asked Walt.

"The guy who went underground? Sure. Made headlines in London when I was there. What's the latest on him?"

"Looks as if he's around," said Oliver. "His family and newspapers too have had letters from him mailed from different parts of the country . . . of course, that's no real indication . . . someone else could have posted them. All the same . . . And the police have offered six thousand rand for information. But so far nothing more than a fine crop of rumours."

"Some say he's disguised in a sari as an Indian woman!" exclaimed Adelaide.

Everyone was highly diverted and I, wondering, *does* Matthew know where he is . . . and if so . . .

I overheard Walt say to Adelaide, " The trials must have caused quite a sensation." She looked comically disbelieving before she said, "But of course, you've only just arrived. No, it's been a struggle to get the press interested."

"Surely the community . . ."

"The Africans? Oh yes, though nowadays we're so cut off we only guess. The whites? Peace and quiet, that's all they care about, no matter how."

I went outside. When I moved from the house I could see the sky, ink-blue, the stars frosty. I looked around at the neighbouring houses. Indifference! I could spit on it, grind it between my teeth. Shit to indifference! I wanted Matthew! Matthew with his committal, his generosity. I wanted him terribly. A bat fluttered by, "Ugh!" Automatically I was revolted, then realized nothing mattered now but my love for Matthew. I felt at once invulnerable and utterably vulnerable.

I stood for a while under the stars. The night was still. And I, quite simply, rejoiced. After a time I went back into the noise and haze of the party and saw, across the room, Matthew talking to Oliver. He felt my glance. Our eyes met. He said something to Oliver and a moment later he was beside me, his hand closing over mine.

"Annie. You know what's happened?" he asked. I nodded. "What foolishness," he said, "the time we've wasted."

Outside we clung to each other, we kissed. Silently we drove to my cottage. Within four walls I felt ridiculously shy until his hands touched and held me, his mouth found mine. Then with tender sensual deliberation he undressed me, pausing to kiss, to say my name, until I lay trembling between the sheets. "These confounded pants!" he mocked his clumsiness. My shaky giggle turned to a sigh as his body came down onto mine . . .

Chapter 11

"DARIUS FORTUNE HAS DISAPPEARED," SAID MATTHEW. "His sister in Pondoland can give no clue . . . or won't. There's no point in trying to find him. Not if he's this afraid."

I asked if Beatrice knew, imagining the dreadful blow to her hopes, the pain at her man's defection.

"Yes. I told her. She said simply that she understood. She hoped he was safe."

There was no alternative now but to call Dan Makhana as a witness. An adjournment was granted for the Defence to negotiate with the State to bring him from Robben Island.

The night before Matthew had to leave for Cape Town, in the act of packing he paused—he had a surprised look on his face—and said, "Annie, how ever did I live without you? To think I kept shoring up my defences! Yes, I was trying to escape; not the way you meant, not through my work, but from something that went badly wrong . . . but I don't believe in raking over the past, the future is ours. With you loving me I feel capable of anything!"

As he shut the suitcase his hands remained, holding down the lid; with the passing of moments it became an indication of unsureness, even apprehension. "My dear, it is dreadful selfishness on my part . . . so much is unpredictable, perilous, I should not involve you . . ."

"It's late, you're tired, so am I," and my hands lifted his from the suitcase, raised one, then the other, to my mouth to kiss.

And in the darkness of the night with the sea sounding, inside the darkness of the cottage with only our murmurs and our heartbeats sounding, we lay in each other's arms, mouth to mouth, each exploring loving the dark of the other and in the darkness brilliance flickered, flared, exploded . . .

Velvet the dark, and in the peace the smell of our sex which somehow sealed our oneness . . . An owl hooted, we smiled, remembering, and kissed, and slept . . .

With morning, the shared present wrenched from us, Matthew flew to Cape Town. Stunned by deprivation, I yet felt stupendously alive. And the next evening I too set out on a journey.

The night grew steadily colder. A tiny chill of fear had settled in my stomach. But senseless to be nervous. It was perfectly legal. Simply a question of visiting Beatrice Qaba's family. Quite legal . . .

The train laboured along the branch line to stop at cheerless stations, each a small cluster of lights in the darkness . . . the Sunday's River and the Bushman's River but a brief reflection of our passing. At last I dozed.

Four A.M. A dim-lit station, small, old-fashioned. The coloured attendant helped me with my overnight bag. "Mind, lady! It's icy cold. Must be snow on the Berg."

I hurried to the exit, down steps to where some cars stood.

"Taxi!"

"Where to, lady?"

"Grand Hotel." Matthew had said, "There'll be a Grand Hotel."

The streetlights emphasized the darkness beyond their range. I sought comfort in the recollection of Matthew's voice: "Beatrice is worried, she's not heard from her family for weeks; besides, you ought to look in on the court there . . ."

We drew up at a balconied building. The driver knocked on the door. Silence. He knocked again. Silence. "Verdomde kaffers!" he grumbled. "Better try the Excelsior." There a black porter led me down a long rackety corridor, unlocked a door, and switched on a feeble light. Too tired to undress, I lay down under the greasy eiderdown . . . and thought of Matthew, where now, in a hotel in Cape Town? Thought of our loving, of the intimate conversations, the quiet, and then the loving again . . .

A dragging clanking broke into my restless sleep . . . the corridor . . . the long dark corridor, the lion in the lav ready to pounce out on me when I had to fetch Mom's knitting . . . the strange room . . . the eiderdown . . .

A loud bell established normality. I washed quickly, applied extra eyeliner for morale, checked my instructions, made a brief telephone call, and went to the dining room. Halfway through breakfast came the dragging clanking . . . a man with a wooden leg heaved across the room.

As I hurried purposefully out to the square, still smiling at the anticlimax, I found myself almost in the arms of a thickset man in a hat. I backed away, strolled casually to the corner, trying to find my sunglasses in my handbag . . . Is he? Could he be? He could . . . my telephone call : . . I forced myself not to look back. I felt conspicuous, my coat too well cut, too short, the colour too bright, my eyeliner . . . where could the dark glasses be? Luckily they were cheap, I was always losing dark glasses . . . Mfaxa, his dark glasses made him even more repellent . . . Kerk Street! Good. The shady side was better cover, but a harsh wind forced me back to the sunny side. I kept close to the buildings. There was only one shop, the rest were warehouses. Will people wonder what I'm doing here? No one ahead. Behind? Is he? Could be. Hell, I feel white and tall —tall? I was passing a small church. I went in. It was empty. I sat in a pew. I tried to rub off the eyeliner. Sparrows fluttered in the rafters. I knelt. I longed for Matthew, said a short incoherent prayer for him and for Beatrice. Nothing much else came to mind. I tried to retrieve the sense of venturing, of discovery . . . I was frozen. My knees ached on the thin hassock. I went back into the frosty sunshine. Ahead was a stretch of rough ground. Beyond were strongly etched flat-topped hills. Dotted with scrub, they had an austere beauty in the clarified light. Matthew had said, "Olive Schreiner is buried on a hill nearby" . . . Boldly I moved on, relieved when the ground's unevenness, the clutter of gray-green weeds, made me concentrate. I stopped to pluck burrs from my stockings.

My landmark, a tall tree, on closer sight became a peppercorn tree, sheltering a low whitewashed house with iron roof. Behind was a larger building, a church, beyond again were several houses, a road . . . and a gray Volkswagen . . . in which I could now descry a heavy-jowled man wearing a hat, beside him an African. They watched my arrival.

To one side of the white house a young man was chopping wood. At sight of me his bony, bearded face contracted into mistrust.

I quickly said, "Beatrice Qaba asked me to come. I telephoned her father." Irrelevantly I wished I had managed the click of the name better. "I'm afraid the S.B. have followed." Was I harming them?

He glanced at the road, scrutinized for a moment the Volkswagen, and his mistrust of me diminished. "My father is in the church. I will fetch him. Please come inside. It is mission ground." He was reassuring me: a white did not need a permit to be here.

"I'm Anne Dawson."

"I am Nathaniel Qaba." How the sight of us shaking hands would aggravate the jowled man!

The front door led into a small room which was a riot of colour, each wall different, like children's sweets, lemon, pink, orange, green, with a blue ceiling.

"What a lovely room!"

" My sister, Beatrice, chose the colours. I painted it. Please . . ." He indicated an overstuffed chair and went to fetch his father.

It was cold. Hanging on the orange wall was a Renoir print. This, too, must be her influence. A dining room suite and two armchairs filled the room. On the sideboard four glasses and a jug stood beside baptism certificates; a plain brass cross hung on the wall . . . a few volumes of Dickens, a Bible, a Methodist hymnal . . .

The door opened again with a draft of icy air and a white-haired clergyman came in, followed by Nathaniel. Samuel Qaba's round black face was unlined. As I rose he took my hand in both of his—his hands were very cold—and he looked into my eyes before saying, "It is good of you to come, madam. Nathaniel tells me you bring word of Beatrice." He gestured me back to my chair and rubbed his hands to warm them. His dark suit was frayed at the cuffs, spotted here and there. "I would have tried to visit her more often," he went on, and sat down near me, "but although she should get two visits a week, unless I get to the jail by five in the morning it is impossible, there is so great a line of people waiting."

"Even then," said Nathaniel, "you're lucky to get a minute or two."

I was appalled at how appreciative Mr. Qaba was of my visit, and relieved to notice he no longer addressed me as "madam." He insisted I have tea while I told them about Beatrice. From their eagerness emanated their feeling for her.

"You know," her father confided, "the Government wants to stop our people speaking English. Well, Beatrice gave lessons at home, she helped the children. Sometimes when I stayed with her in the township I would fear the authorities might dismiss her, or detain her . . . in the nights we would be awake, listening to noises, wondering if it was them. But when they came for her, I was not there . . ."

"She was anxious about you," I told Nathaniel. "She heard you were expelled from college."

"He is too outspoken," said the old man proudly.

"She must not worry!" Nathaniel's face contorted until it was like a skull. "Tell her I'm fine! I'm here! About to get a job . . . as a teacher!"

"Are you?"

"No," he said ferociously. "And no! And no!"

I was startled by the sophistication of his reply.

The old man explained. "He has only a temporary permit to be here with me . . . you know the Section Ten."

Nathaniel—his eyes blazed—was laughing. "As for a job! *If* I should get a permit to remain!"

"This is an area of terrible poverty," said his father. "Last week many children had no food. It is wonderful, a family can get so used to going without food that they can exist on one meal a day." His hands gestured despair. "The mothers come to me. 'What can we do?' they ask. I feel very terrible. I cannot say, 'You must pray.' How can I say that? How?"

"What about that relief organization?" I was aware that my voice sounded English, glib.

"Ha!" Nathaniel clearly thought so too. "For the authorities there is no starvation, therefore no need for relief."

The old man said, "We hoped for Nathaniel to become a

doctor. You know how our youth are restricted by law. But still we dared to dream . . . And now . . . it is fortunate he is not arrested."

Nathaniel broke in impatiently. "There was an English professor who came lately to Fort Hare to lecture. He encouraged, he could understand . . ."

"Was his name Gibbon?"

"You know him! Well, he said it may be possible to help with a bursary to England."

His father was nodding agreement, but sadly. "If Nathaniel is to go they would never give him a passport. If he leaves without one, they will never allow him to return. And in England, what will his life be? I do not know, but can he make a life *here?*" The old man sighed. "Sometimes I ask God how . . ."

Banging on the door silenced him.

"Viljoen!" Nathaniel growled the name.

His father opened the door and, with courtesy, faced the heavy man in the hat, whose black assistant lurked at his heels.

"Good morning, Mr. Viljoen?"

Viljoen looked past him at me. "Have you a permit?" he asked roughly.

"I understood there was no need."

"Mr. Viljoen, there must be some mistake. This is mission land," the old man was firm.

Viljoen took his time. He looked us over, then looked around the room. "Well, that'll soon be stopped," he finally said. "And you, Samuel," he jabbed a thick finger at Mr. Qaba's chest, "you will be shifted to where you belong.

The location! Yes." He looked at the ceiling. "Yes, you just watch your step!" He strode off, leaving the door open.

Watching him go, "We are *men*," said the old man, half to himself. "And we have our feelings." He shut the door. His voice began to tremble with anger. "It's when he comes into the church! He has no manners. He comes, cigarette in mouth! When he goes, cigarette ends lie about in the aisles. It is a desecration!"

"You once were a member of the African National Congress, weren't you?" I asked. We needed to change the subject.

"Yes. Until it grew too wild. Defying laws, you know. That was in 1952 . . . Perhaps I was wrong. Certainly there was a great time under Lutuli, in 1959. Yes," his voice was alert with the memory, "I joined in the thirties. The great depression, a time of famine. We agitated for better wages. We went to Parliament in Cape Town to appeal to the Minister." He chuckled to recall that hey-day.

"And where did that get us?" said Nathaniel sarcastically.

"Yes, we were too moderate, I know, I know. Yet where has the sabotage got us?" Clearly it was a continuing clash between them.

"Ha!" Nathaniel. "The sabotage, feeble! What could you expect—Mandela, Makhana—they are the old guard! We need new leaders, young, tough!"

"Mr. Qaba," I interrupted, "you left the Congress but you were imprisoned after Sharpeville?"

"A bitter time. Yet I regarded it as an honour. To be with all those young men." He smiled at Nathaniel. "But bitter.

I was forced—it was midwinter, you know, as cold as now—and we had to stand naked in the yard while they decontaminated—that was the worst time . . . But that is of the past. Beatrice, now," his face and voice were grave, "this is what matters."

I had dreaded this moment. As gently as I could I told them there was not much hope of an acquittal. Painfully I remembered Matthew's anxiety, hastily said, "But Matthew Marais asked me to tell you he will certainly appeal."

After I'd explained I was making a study of the trials and must go to the local courthouse, Mr. Qaba drove me there in his rusty old Morris and I told him something about Matthew . . . blissful agony to say the name, as if I were not repeating over and over in my mind, Matthew my love my love I love you . . .

I told Mr. Qaba too about the tweedy woman—I wanted to leave him with some cheerful memory—and how Matthew had routed Lubbe, how Beatrice was again getting the food every day. He laughed to think of it, and was grateful.

When we drew up outside a granite building, "Beatrice will be so glad to have news of you," I said, and this time I held his hand in both of mine, and said foolishly, "Please look after yourself."

How long before he was arrested again? They might take him in for the hell of it, to remind him what would happen if he went back to the struggle . . . As for Nathaniel, I had offered to write to Keith Gibbon.

Two white men who had paused to stare walked on.

Inside was a formal court, with a spruce Magistrate on a

high bench and a crowded dock—the numbers decently pinned to the front panel. The public gallery was empty, only a youngster sat in the press box. The atmosphere was chilly, sunless, efficient. In the witness box stood a man; facing him, the black-gowned Prosecutor.

". . . he lied, Your Worship."

"Ah, Abraham, why should he do that?" The Prosecutor had a streaming cold.

"This man and me, Your Worship, we are neighbours. I have a patch of lawn. He keeps a donkey, and this donkey, Your Worship, is always urinating on my lawn. So I threatened to take him to court . . ."

"So you're saying, Abraham, that because of this argument he told lies about you to the police?"

"Yes . . ."

The Magistrate had to rub his hands warm . . . reminding me of Samuel Qaba's chapped hands. Should I send gloves? What size? By registered post, that would be safe . . . I concentrated again on the trial.

The State case was that twenty-nine men, among them the eight in the dock, had plotted to invade a dorp three years earlier. Numbers 1 and 6 were brothers. The latter now faced the Prosecutor. How odd! Pale-skinned with sleek hair, accused Number 6 might have been Spanish, while the Prosecutor, thin and dark-skinned, had the tightly curled hair of a coloured man.

Number 6. Eighteen years old, name of Jerry Mondlu. His thinly clad body attempted bravado, but his hands perpetually kneaded each other.

"State witnesses numbers 1 and 4 say you recruited

them?"

"No, it is not true, Your Worship."

". . . that you said," and the Prosecutor read from his notes, " 'Our leader Sobukwe is in jail. We must fight! We must not let the whites own our country.' "

"It is not true."

"That at a meeting in the veld—the jungle, as you call it —you forced them to take the oath?" He blew his nose like a trumpet.

"No, Your Worship."

"Remember, Jerry, I asked, 'How were you supposed to fight? In Parliament?' and State witness number 4 said, 'We must kill the whites. Even young children.' Yes, Jerry, and then he said we must have guns, pangas, axes, weapons which would come from Russia and Ghana?"

"No, it was all lies, Your Worship," Jerry's voice flagged.

"Everything is lies?" The Prosecutor's voice was gentle.

"Yes, Your Worship."

"Your name, your address?"

"No! I mean all that is to do with the invasion is not true."

"Ah! So now you admit some things?" Then in a swirl of fury, "Listen to me, Jeremiah! Listen!" and, between mops at his nose with a large blue handkerchief, he questioned, "What about Sharpeville, when Saracens were out?"

"1960?" Jerry looked uncertain.

"Yes. You were a boy, a young boy. It impressed you deeply, hey?" Now the Prosecutor's voice rose. "You saw all the police, the Saracen armoured cars . . . Yes, you were so young, eeeh eeeh eeeh . . ."—in mimicry of a childish voice. Court officials laughed loudly. The Magistrate was silent.

Jerry, serious-faced, protested. "But I spoke in my same voice then. I did not squeak." His brother, Number 1, looked strained.

"And you knew of Bantu who burned their passes?"

"I heard. I would never burn mine. I need it, to keep my job."

"You need a pass to get a job?"

"Yes, Your Worship."

"To get a house?"

"Yes."

"You need your pass if you go to the bank?"

"Yes."

"And if you want to go to another town?"

"Yes, Your Worship."

"So the pass is a burden?"

"No, Your Worship, not for me. It helps me."

The heads of the other accused followed the abrupt exchanges.

"The white man is baas, is that not so, Jerry?"

"Yes."

"And you, as Bantu, can live only in the location?"

"Yes."

"As Bantu, you cannot go in the bioscope?"

"Yes. No, Your Worship." Jerry sounded dazed.

His brother's eyes were wild.

The Prosecutor took his time, blew his nose several times. "And you cannot go in the tea rooms?"

"No."

I could no longer look at the brother, at his frantic impotence.

"You Bantu have an inferior education?"

"Yes."

"What's that? Speak up!"

"Yes, Your Worship."

"En jy is dood tevrede?" The Prosecutor must have been carried away; quickly he corrected himself. "I mean, you are dead happy with your lot, Jerry?"

"Dead happy, Your Worship." The voice was small.

"Dead happy in your job?"

"Dead happy. I get my pay."

Jerry's round boyish face was quite blank, but his knuckles gleamed white in his tense hands. All of a sudden his hands went limp. I realized the Magistrate had spoken. Adjournment!

I walked to the station. Each step was an escape from degradation. To witness, and not to protest—was this not to participate?

As I hurried along the road two Africans came level with me, and passed . . . one was elderly, carrying a box of provisions, the other wearing jeans, young, tall, with a springy stride. I caught a snatch of the conversation, heard the words which poured from the young man's sharp face. He was speaking Afrikaans!

"En jy is dood tevrede?"

The train for Port Elizabeth, remarkably, was on time. In the empty coupé I unpacked my nightdress and toothbrush, then found at the bottom of the bag the sunglasses I'd mislaid.

Jerked in and out of sleep by the train's constant halts, half waking, half dreaming, I moved along the clifftop road, a neighbour's mongrel at my heels, past me moved the old man with the provisions, and his young companion with the springy stride—his gait somehow in suspense as in slow motion—and though what he said was soundless, I knew it to be Afrikaans, and I yelled at him: "Where is your manhood?" only my voice was without sound too. They moved on along the cliff road and I, and the dog, on too, then I ran fast down the steep steps to the small beach and into the sea, calm and cold. I floated on the surface of the water. The mongrel tried to clamber onto me as if I were a raft. I thrust it off and lay, starfish-spread. Above, at the top of the steps, a tall black figure appeared, and stood, far above yet near. I looked around. The beach was empty. My eyes were drawn back to the steps. There was no one there. Unease, like a breath of air, brushed me. Was it the young man with the springy step? Had he heard my soundless yell? I ran from the sea and huddled my towel about me and lay on sand warmed by the day's sun . . . A barking and whining and the mongrel stood rigid, bristling, on the beach. Its yelping attracted strangers who moved down the steps across the beach toward a body, sprawled, profile turned inward, while from one side a dark brown patch clotted the fine sand. In the shallows of the sea the young man was washing the knife clean. Then he replaced it in a pocket of his jeans and turned slowly toward the crowd with an expression which could have been an intimation of happiness . . . "dood tevrede." He was wearing a pair of cheap sunglasses . . . On my lifeless face I observed a small smile

of irony which, as they lifted my body, collapsed into
vacuity . . .

Chapter 12

T HE PLANE ARRIVED PUNCTUALLY AT 8 A.M. I WAS IN Matthew's arms again, exactly six days from the moment he'd left.

By 9.45 A.M. we were in a village eighty miles away, waiting on the veranda of the modern yellow-brick courthouse to which the trial had been transferred to accommodate a military incursion. A prison van with military escort drew up. Officers with revolvers and soldiers with Stenguns jumped smartly from the escort vehicles to surround the van as a policeman unlocked it. A man climbed out. At once soldiers and police closed in to march him to the cells across the road.

Matthew was already intercepting them, to shake the prisoner by the hand and accompany him. Dr. Daniel Makhana. He was not very tall, a slight man, gray-haired, in shabby sports coat and flannels; in the hustle his movements remained leisurely and, as they waited outside the cells for the door to be unlocked, he turned to joke with Matthew.

Walt Tree joined me and made some comment. I did not hear, was too moved to speak. I could hardly believe that this man was in prison for the rest of his life . . . it was absurd. Watching him with Matthew, his old friend, I thought about the precious moments for them. In these times, caring for someone who suffered or was in danger turned each hour, each minute, that you could be with them into a positive extension to life; life became instantly and continuously valuable . . . however brief and business-like their discussion had to be when—besides its being bugged—they had to consider the expense for the defense . . .

"No wonder it's costing the earth," Walt commented . . . the Prosecutor, Lubbe, and Smit had been reinforced by several white S.B.'s and a stout colonel, and a covey of black colleagues hovered around Mfaxa, who suddenly detached himself, came over to the press box, and accosted Walt.

"You pressmen, you say bad things about us policemen. What do you have against us?" And he bared his teeth in a jovial smile.

After he'd gone, "Guy gives me the heebie-jeebies," Walt confided.

"He and Lubbe," I said, "to think they've probably got wives, children . . ."

Matthew appeared in the doorway. Our eyes met in a brief, sober glance, nothing to indicate the secret exquisite joy, the heightened awareness of our loving alliance in face of all these police. With him was a local attorney.

Beatrice Qaba had arrived. Matthew escorted her to the dock. She looked lonelier, seated in this modern spacious courtroom, but at least it was more comfortable, and surely she must draw strength from Dan Makhana's arrival.

"Rise in court!"

Did the Magistrate look a shade less mournful on the loftier bench?

Matthew spoke, "I call the witness, Daniel Makhana."

He came in, flanked by two policemen, with soldiers behind; about him, a weariness like fine dust. His wrists were handcuffed. He blinked to adjust after the sunlight, then with unperturbed gaze took in Matthew, and, with the smallest flicker of amusement, the State line-up.

The colonel ordered the escort to unlock the handcuffs; there was a bustling as uniformed men came and went. The key was lost! Makhana stood, arms at ease, wrist to wrist, no need to grin to show his enjoyment.

In front of Walt, the plump woman in the pot hat spoke up, "Try one of these." And cheerfully she proffered a bulging bunch of keys. A policeman thankfully took them, began to try one after another. She turned to us with a winning smile. "You have to lock everything, but *everything*, the servants you get these days!" Walt was charmed.

The Magistrate's patience stretched on. Suddenly a click. Makhana's hands came free. He went into the witness box.

Before Matthew could speak the Prosecutor was up. "U Edelagbaar, Your Worship, my information is that the defense has not yet paid for the transportation here of this witness. The State asks that until this is settled, the witness should not be called upon."

Matthew was consulting the attorney. "Your Worship,"

he said, "my instructions are that the payment will be made tomorrow."

The Prosecutor began to protest. The Magistrate's patience snapped. "I accept the assurance. Proceed, Mr. Marais."

"Your Worship"—we could sense that Lubbe was egging the Prosecutor on—"the State wishes to request that the press withdraw. It is not in the interests of the State that this man's evidence should be reported. He is an important political prisoner."

Matthew was up, aggressively angry. "Your Worship, I am amazed!" but as he protested, argued—"It is against every tenet of justice . . . expert evidence on a key factor . . . a tradition that court proceedings be publicly reported . . ."—we knew it was hopeless.

"Yes, well," the Magistrate fingered his moustache, "the court grants the application. Will the press leave the court?"

Walt was fuming. I only had time to cast a glance of furious disappointment at Matthew and to observe that Makhana had remained unperturbed, before we were shepherded out. On the veranda we found Lubbe. Protest burst from us, one after another—the keen young man, the woman, and Walt in an authoritative drawl: "Unprecedented!" "Unheard of!" "Nowhere else!" ending with: "The whole world will think you're afraid of Dr. Makhana!"—my shrill assertion. The colonel had overheard. He looked us up and down. "It is not in the interests of the State. That is all there is to it!"

The others went disgustedly off to file their stories. The colonel and Lubbe returned to the court.

I sat on the edge of the veranda in the sun thinking about Makhana, his imperturbability . . . but I could understand what Matthew had told me, that one of the things Makhana found most onerous on the Island was having to wear "boy's" shorts . . . The sun had grown quite warm. I remembered again that time with Matthew when, sleep-coupled, we'd awakened and I, then he, began drowsily to reminisce . . . "D'you know when I fell in love—when you gave me that small stone, on the heights . . . 'iets antwoord, iets glo . . .' Your voice was quite delectable!" "No, Annie, no, when we heard the owl, that was the auspicious moment." "No, before that . . ." But I found I could not talk of the time when he showed me Ramchandran's note; quickly I said, "When you told me about the minestrike." But he knew, and leaned to kiss me on the brow before, firmly, "No. It was when we sheltered from the rain. You'd been looking cross and suddenly your green eyes were happy."

A door banged. Lubbe headed for me. He was about to confront me when he skidded on the last step. His face went puce.

"Your passport!"

I fumbled in my bag, and handed it to him. Fear wired through me. He glared at the first page, searched in his pockets. "Here!" I tore a page from my notebook and offered my pen, in quick gestures so that my hands should not tremble. As soon as he'd noted my name and address I said, "May I have it back?" I was not obliged to tell more. He glowered, returned it with the pen, and abruptly went back to the courtroom.

How odd. Was he so put out by slipping? Had he not fully realized my connection with Matthew? Certainly, since Walt's arrival, he'd seen me as much in his company and our easy relationship might have deceived him . . . Feeble of me to offer paper and pen, but perhaps it disconcerted . . . My agitation took time to subside. . .

From the court came the escort, surrounding Makhana, followed by a group of Special Branch. He saw me and as he was led past he smiled. I smiled back. We were narrowly observed by the S.B. Suddenly I saw what frightened men they were—looking from Makhana to me and back; the colonel, even Lubbe . . . frightened of this man, this prisoner, who looked tired but whose spirit clearly would not be broken. Frightened of me? It saddened me . . . their fear.

"What did Dan Makhana say?" Walt asked Matthew as we piled into his car to go to a drive-in for a quick lunch. Matthew's hand held mine for a moment, hard, then he started up the car.

"I expect you remember, there was a peaceful strike of Africans in 1961; the Government brought out massive force to crush it. That was the last straw. Dan's evidence centered on those events. It was he, with Mandela and other leaders, who then decided to abandon their policy of non-violence . . . to turn to sabotage. This was at the end of May. Out of the question that Beatrice could have advocated violence in March. He spoke with devastating authority.

"But the really splendid moment," Matthew laughed at the recollection, "was when the Prosecutor tried to get Dan to implicate his comrades. 'That would be contrary to my principles,' Dan said. 'Principles!' the Prosecutor said. 'What about your oath before the Almighty, to tell the whole truth?' Then Dan asked in an innocent voice, 'Are the police working for the Almighty then? That I do not know about.' "

"Matthew, any chance of getting food to him?" I asked.

"I've spoken to the colonel. He's agreed!"

I went off to shop. Afterward, in the clean air, under the sun, hurrying back with my mind on Matthew, on his happiness that his friend should have this small treat, I found myself singing . . . Steak, fruit, I showed him what I'd bought. A celebration for Dan, he said, after more than a year of mealiepap and "boy's" meat.

Beatrice Qaba was in the witness box. Matthew kept his examination concise and she answered with composure, confirming that the van had belonged to Darius Fortune; because he'd gone away she'd completed the sale. She denied it was for the A.N.C.

I'd wondered about how much she had been involved, and had asked Oliver—I knew Matthew could not answer such a question—if he thought she had actually been connected with the A.N.C. "She'd be a witless woman if she hadn't been," he'd said. "It's a measure of self-respect. But I have no doubt whatsoever that the S.B. concocted much of the case—they know she supports Congress and they hate her pluck and independence."

Now Matthew asked her, "This meeting in March 1961, did you attend?"

"No, Your Worship."

Perhaps it was the way the light fell on her, a sculptural process which planed her heavy-lidded eyes, her broad nose and full mouth, creating levels of light and dark that were beautiful . . . How had I ever felt pity? Her quiet strength rejected pity as contemptible patronage. She moved her head slightly and was again plain Beatrice Qaba . . . no, there was some subtle change . . .

"What sort of meetings did you attend in 1961?"

"There was the welfare committee."

"Did it hold any meetings in March 1961?"

"It's such a long time ago . . . I know there were meetings, but I can't recall just when exactly, Your Worship," and she turned to the Magistrate apologetically.

Which was more intolerable, to watch her, caught in the web spun by Mfaxa and the others, or to watch Matthew toiling to free her? His intelligence, integrity, and tenacity no match for their power and corruption, his optimism continually having to be regenerated . . .

Finally: "And did you ever raise funds for explosives, guns, for weapons of any kind?" Matthew asked.

"No, Your Worship."

The Prosecutor rose. Beatrice tensed. Mfaxa smiled like a benefactor.

"If Your Worship pleases. So, Beatrice, you don't recall any details of those welfare meetings?"

"Very little, Your Worship."

"It seems you have a very bad memory, Beatrice. You didn't hear of the new plan?"

"No."

"Come, come, Beatrice. It wasn't illegal just to *hear* of it."

She looked startled.

"Very peculiar, someone as intelligent as a schoolteacher, not to know about such a thing . . ." If Matthew ever indulged in sarcasm the Magistrate immediately jumped.

It was warm inside the court but Beatrice had drawn her coat close about her . . . The magnitude of what was going on . . . my forebears had prepared the ground . . . I was one of this corrupt society, sitting here, allowing it to happen, my puny little exposure in a remote London newspaper was laughable . . . Yet I had to go on, I, too, reduced to play my part . . . feeling big whenever I smiled at Beatrice; and when Walt and I joked together, or bought magazines, thinking: there, we're not do-gooders, we're normal, human . . . My head had begun to ache . . . what must Matthew feel?

The tea break was short—the Magistrate wanted to finish with Beatrice by evening. When court reassembled, Matthew, his face white, rose. "Your Worship, a matter of gravity! The accused has been subjected to intimidation. During the break Sergeant Mfaxa told a colleague, in front of Beatrice Qaba, that unless she looked out she might find other members of her family implicated." He did not trouble to disguise his contemptuous anger. Mfaxa sat sucking his teeth.

The Magistrate cleared his throat. "The Security Police, I am sure, Mr Marais, are performing their duty honourably, and any slight misunderstanding will be satisfactorily cleared up."

The atmosphere could be cut with a knife.

Walt muttered. "What's the use of Matthew trying? Only makes the creeps loathe him the more. If that's possible." I tried to shut down on panic.

The Prosecutor was up. "It is shameful, my learned friend, casting unseemly aspersions . . ."

They were insatiable . . . I could see Beatrice had been affected . . . she spoke unconvincingly through routine cross-examination.

Now Lubbe was whispering to the Prosecutor.

"Beatrice," the Prosecutor's tone was ingratiating, "when did you last see your brother, Nathaniel?"

"Nathaniel?" She was badly discomposed.

"You heard me! Don't play for time! When?"

Matthew was up, but his complaint at the Prosecutor's curtness was overridden.

"Well, Beatrice?"

"I am not absolutely certain . . . I think it must have been a few days before I was arrested."

"Yes, where?"

She looked rattled. "He would come, sometimes, to visit me. But as I say, I cannot quite recall . . ."

"How is it you remember some things, not others?"

"With respect, Your Worship, you also perhaps remember some things and forget others."

"Don't you question me! I am asking the questions! Now. Did you not see Nathaniel at a neighbor's . . . at Jolobe's house, perhaps?"

"No, Your Worship! I do not believe my brother was ever in that house."

Walt whispered, "How long before Nathaniel's in the dock? With Jolobe State witness number one."

I got up and walked casually from the court, stood for a moment in the sun on the veranda as if bored with the proceedings, then strolled up the main street . . . Nathaniel, he must be warned. Matthew had told me about the possibilities for getting him out of the country . . . he must be saved from this merciless bulldozing . . .

As I made my way to the post office I remembered the day—only two days after I'd visited him and his father—when Nathaniel had turned up at my cottage. A sequence of images and emotions crowded me . . . Nathaniel over lunch, sullen, lapsing into monosyllables . . . Nathaniel, sinewy, assertive, his bare feet sinking into the wet sand as we walked along the shore. "It meant something, what my sister taught, true's God! Kids would come to her house. I guess even the informers were won over." Then, as he heaved a rock into the sea, "Impimpis! Informers! What has been done to my people!" And my horror as he talked of his cousin and the ten children in the house where he was staying in the township. "Her husband's in jail for eight years, her mother's in for three and a half—so she has her own baby and seven brothers and sisters to look after. Then there's two kids of a friend who's in for eighteen months. One and two and seven—ten, see?" And when I asked if they were all in jail on political charges, his angry shrug. "You can lock us up! You can destroy our families! You can not stop us thinking!" Suddenly he erupted into hectic vitality. "I had a jazz combo once, not bad either! But two of them are on the Island now," and he rolled up his trouser legs and tiptoed into the sea, to retreat rapidly, exaggerating his shivers, making me laugh. "Come on, teatime," I said. His face slid into a grin, "Man, Miss Dawson, what I couldn't do to a can of beer!" "OK. I'll break the law for you. And for goodness' sake call me Anne!" It was at this moment that we came upon a family fishing in a rock pool. They stopped to stare. After we'd passed I could feel them, watching askance the white woman in laughing conversation with a non-white . . .

Arrived at the post office I found the telephone was free. I made a discreet call.

When I got back to court Beatrice was saying, "They searched my house time and again. Sergeant Mfaxa and others . . . they took my letters, my books. Even the picture I had of Chief Lutuli."

"A picture?"

"Three times I had to get a new one. Each time they came and took it . . ."

Matthew worked until late that night on his summing up. Twice I made him coffee. When, finally, he called out, "It's done!" and I joined him while he put his notes and files in order for the morning, I was surprised and touched to see that he looked peaceful.

"Let's get some air," he suggested, "or are you too tired?"

I put my coat on. He tucked my arm in his and held me close to his side as we made our way across the rocks. The beach, white in the moonlight, stretched for miles to the north. We moved on the fringe of a silvered sea. Never had it seemed so brilliant, the sky too, such a glorious night, and suddenly we were running and laughing and shouting and our long moon-cast shadows jigged crazily about the white sands until, breathless, we had to slow down.

"What would I do without you?" he asked, still laughing, and held me fast for a moment before we strode on.

I remembered earlier, the nausea of anger and fear, and "How do you cope?"—I wanted him to clarify the confusion of my emotions.

"By taking part in one of these trials I give credence to the lie that justice exists, that the courts are respectable. D'you see what I'm getting at? Simply by defending Beatrice, I'm playing their game. They claim to the world: we are a free country, look at our courts! But it has to be done, Annie. This is it. It is our country. And we're going to win, my dear. How ever arduous the struggle."

And now I saw quite clearly that involvement in the trials was tied up with one's passion for the place, and vice versa—how had Alan put it, "scraps of humanity . . ." that morning before he'd taken me to meet Matthew . . . an age ago, a different world . . .

"A long day tomorrow," Matthew said and kissed me. We headed home.

"When does Dan leave?" I asked.

"In the morning. I'll go early to the cells to see him."

"How do they keep their spirits high?" I was thinking of the positive strength of Dan Makhana.

Matthew paused to light his pipe. "Dan says it's impossible to convey the true feel. There are days on the Island when the warders are 'greedy for violence.' Day after day of harsh routine. Gray concrete. Hard labor, breaking stones in the quarries, breaking rocks along the shore . . . He said how much the short hours of study mean to them. Above all, there's the comradeship, the belief that the future is theirs. 'The knowledge,' as Dan put it, 'that we shall be free.' "

And then as we walked on I remembered the schoolmaster who'd served his sentence on the Island and who'd told Shula that at night, when they were locked into their cells, after lights out, when a man had no appearances to keep up, you heard a sigh. A sigh in the dark which seemed to run from cell to cell.

The sea surged and retreated and surged and retreated as we moved along its edge.

"I don't see how they manage," I said. "Men like Dan, in prison for life. How they hold on to that belief. And you, that you believe . . ."

Matthew's pipe had gone out. He stopped to relight it. I watched his face in the flare of the match and wished I had not spoken.

"How do you imagine one goes on unless one believes?" He moved so rapidly now it was an effort to keep up. "Did you know Jashbai? . . . I knew him well. A durable young chap you'd have said, sound. When he was being interrogated he managed to get a message to his wife: 'Pray for me' it said. He was not a religious man, Annie. Three days later he fell from the seventh floor of the Special Branch office. So they said. Or was he pushed to his death?" Matthew's voice shook. I was holding his hand harder and harder. "How do you think one lives with that? With the knowledge of Dan, the others . . . Without believing? Oh no, they suffer for a better future . . . Jashbai died for a better future . . . I believe that! And it will be. Without doubt, it will be, Annie!"

Chapter 13

T HE LAST ROUND, WE WERE BACK IN THE SUNNY COURT-
room which could have been a schoolroom.

The Prosecutor, his hair brushed high, his face bright with
confidence, attacked the main Defence witness. "Daniel, that
Old Testament character," he called him. How could his
evidence be seriously regarded? He was in prison for life;
perjury meant nothing. His sole concern was to further the
aims of his organization, and its policy was that members
should not incriminate each other; so obviously he would
deny that Beatrice Qaba was a member, only confirming
the probability that she *was*, and therefore, guilty as
charged. On the other hand—he gestured expansively—
the State witnesses had absolutely no motive for lying. Two
were already in jail—what possible motive could they have?

He gave a dissertation on violence leading to what he
called the "criminal activities" of Beatrice as exposed in the
trial. That an educated woman, a teacher with the minds of
young Bantu at her mercy, should engage in activity dan-

gerous to the State, was a particularly vicious aspect which he begged the court to hold in mind. He sat down, his job thoroughly done, his conscience conspicuously clear. Walt remarked, "Say, did you hear, he's promoted to be a magistrate?"

Beatrice, now that the ordeal of the witness box was over, was again composed, listening attentively.

Matthew rose. His face—his body too—was taut, yet he spoke without notes, with firm clarity. "Your Worship, the State case depends on the evidence of a series of witnesses whose performance I can only describe as lamentable." Carefully he analyzed each man's record and evidence . . . what was the use? Nothing he said could make any difference. I was trying to will encouragement and strength into him, his face had become ashen . . . "Why then, did these men give this evidence? My learned friend maintains they had no motive to lie because some of them were already in jail. His logic escapes me. No motive? On the contrary, could they not imagine, indeed expect, some reward if they pleased the State?"

Walt sighed. "Great, just great, next he'll accuse them to their faces of cooking it all!"

"As for Dr. Daniel Makhana, it would be naïve not to concede that he would welcome the opportunity to put the true facts on record . . ."

Beatrice did not take her eyes off Matthew.

He paused, stood for a moment in deep reflection. "Daniel Makhana," he continued, "is a doctor, a man who has sacrificed his family life, his home, and his profession, for his ideals, out of a profound sense of responsibility to his people. How ever much the State and you, Your Worship, may disagree with those ideals, you must concede that such ideals have shone like a torch in the dark record of man's history, and in our world today they are regarded as the noblest ideals a man can serve."

I wished Makhana could have heard, could have returned to Robben Island with the passion of Matthew's voice living in his memory . . .

The character of Beatrice Qaba, the evidence of the missionary concerning her work—Matthew dwelt on these, and then: "Your Worship, an essential consideration is—might the Defence case reasonably be true ? It has to be no higher than that. I submit that the State has not proved its case. I ask that the accused, Beatrice Qaba, be acquitted."

He sat down. The last echo of the recording machine crackled into silence. Irrelevantly I marvelled that he'd got through without interruption from the trains. Beatrice held her head high. He turned to her in a gesture of communication. Then he looked out of the window, his hand stroking his chin. Outside, the sun lit up a fruit tree. Nobody stirred . . .

Until the Magistrate, with two mighty tugs at his moustache, spoke. At first, a flow of rhetoric. Eventually: "I found the accused an unsatisfactory witness. It is true that Mani gave confusing evidence but I am satisfied that in the main the State witnesses were reliable . . ." There could be no doubt of his conclusion.

"Beatrice Qaba!"

The policeman whispered to her to stand up. She did, her hands clasping her coat together, her expression one of absolute control. Matthew had turned to look directly at her.

"Beatrice Qaba, the court finds you guilty on all three counts: membership in an unlawful organization, raising funds for its purposes, and attending its meetings. The court bears in mind the long—to my mind, far too long—period for which you were imprisoned awaiting trial. This shall be deducted . . ."

The sentence: four years. Another two and a half years for Beatrice to serve.

Having frowned through his last words on the subject, the Magistrate could withdraw to his small room, could drive back to Port Elizabeth with the Prosecutor, with the Special Branch.

Matthew went at once to Beatrice. "We'll appeal, of course."

"Oh, Mr. Marais," she interrupted before he could say more, "you must not take it to heart. You did your very best. You were fine, just great," and she folded her hands over his. "But they were determined you should not win. And you must know there is no justice in these courts, not for black people."

I shamelessly eavesdropped. She spoke not despairingly but firmly, with cynicism. The policeman was urging her to go. She moved closer to Matthew's side, to add quietly: "It is time we black people faced up to that. I have learned a great deal from this trial, Mr. Marais. And I thank you not only for all your kindness and courage, and how hard you have worked, but for the way you have been to me. It will be a strength in these years ahead."

She clambered for the last time into the prison van waiting in the yard. Sergeant Mfaxa locked her in before hopping up beside the driver. As the van rumbled off we waved good-bye to Beatrice Qaba. She smiled and waved back.

Part Three

Chapter 14

I FELT MY BRAIN WOULD EXPLODE. MY MOUTH WAS DRY
though I'd just had tea. My hands sweated as I gripped
pen and pad and strove to encompass the reality of Beatrice Qaba's trial. I grappled with the quotations I'd marked
only to find I was driving frustration to the pitch of defeat.
Nausea mounted. I can't do it! I'm not up to it! I tore the
pages across and across, stuffed the pieces into an airsickness
bag, and glared from the plane window into the black
night. I'm bored bored bored to screaming with people's
problems! I wish we'd crash . . .

The touchdown was smooth. And owing to a tail wind
we were ahead of time. No sign then of Matthew, who'd
got the last seat on the morning plane and was due to fetch
me. Out of the darkness I stepped into the terminal building, brightly lighted, where the debris of travelers ebbed
and flowed. I found an empty chair and sat, in limbo.
Forced myself to become detached as I watched the bodies
surge around . . . walking on their hind legs, why does
their fur stop growing just there? Why on the naked stretch
of skin those funny dabs of fur? Why an eye on each side

of a nose? A nose with its two holes? How excessively odd
a mouth is . . . why the lips? Until one broke from the
herd to assert his humanity, his familiarity.

"Annie. Come on. Home."

A high hedge, trees and lawn, a small angled house, a
living room plain but for the books. Mary, his housekeeper,
made me feel welcome . . . A large room, almost empty
of furniture, a stack of newspapers in one corner. Bed, and
"I just feel burned out," I said. He fetched some brandy.
"Drink this." At last I slept.

I woke to dim light filtering through the curtains. Depression started and threatened to swamp me. A finger
touched my cheek, stroked a light pattern of tenderness
. . . Matthew, present, awake; the knowledge routed de-
pondency. And suddenly I felt drowning in desire. My
eyes told him. He looked absurdly happy. With kisses he
closed my eyes . . .

I surfaced into panic: that I should love so good a man,
that I could cause his happiness. And saw how vulnerable
he was. I must do nothing, ever, to hurt him . . . I would
not, no I could not! "In Italy where I stayed one summer,"
I said, "there was this nanny goat, with yellow, dark-
circled eyes. It belonged to the neighbours, contadini. They
handled it firmly, they allowed no nonsense. But my visitors were scared because it had a reputation for butting."
Dreamily I was remembering just how it was. "However,
I would look straight into its knowing yellow eyes and I
felt we liked each other. So I gave it a nice ripe fig—the fig
trees were absolutely crammed—and it adored that. I gave
some more. I even dared to offer them in the palm of my

hand and it nuzzled and nibbled. It farted a bit afterward. Anyway, this exchange of gazes and figs became quite a ritual. Then it began to fart a lot. And then it just died . . . brown and blown up, it lay under an olive tree, and the sun burning all around . . . You see!" I wailed, "I killed something I loved!"

Matthew found it extremely funny. "Poor you," he said.

"The poor goat," I protested, but now I was laughing too, more and more.

"Poor scapegoat," he murmured and our mood soared. "Annie," he said when he got some breath, "I wish I'd known you when you were a kid."

"Matthew!" I sat up in horror. "That poor goat never had a kid!"

Eventually we were still. We could hear the birds. The sun had risen. Beatrice Qaba filled my mind, this sunrise, in some cell . . . we didn't yet know in which jail. And suddenly it all overflowed. Matthew had me in his arms. I clung to him like a baby monkey to its parent and he rocked me . . .

Soon after breakfast I had an appointment, planned by Matthew with care. I took a bus into town and all the way I watched. I did not want to make things worse for her, for Dan Makhana's wife. There was risk in her meeting anyone, she was banned from gatherings and this might be so construed, but she was so eager for news. It was a Saturday morning and the streets were crowded. As far as I could tell no one followed—and I stopped again to peer into a shopwindow, in case I could detect a suspicious reflection—

but how to tell? Most of the white men who passed looked like S.B. anyway . . . I reached the bank, strolled in, and waited with, I hoped, a casual air.

She arrived, a little late. She was small like a robin, yet with dignity. We shook hands. I was very moved to see her. I looked around, trying to estimate whether she was followed. It seemed not. We went to a corner beyond Foreign Exchange where fewer people could hear.

"How is Dan?" She sounded breathless.

"Fine. He was just fine," I said. "Strong." Her face glowed as I told her all I could. She was thrilled about the steak, and proud when I quoted what Matthew had said about Dan to the Magistrate.

She was about to go down for a visit. A thousand miles by train to Cape Town, then the ferry boat to Robben Island. And half an hour with Dan. And then a thousand miles back again, to wait another three months. And then another half hour.

"But the worst thing is the barrier," she said in her confiding manner. "I can only see a scrap of his face at a time. One eye, a bit of his mouth. It is hard, Miss Dawson, too cruel, we just want to see each other, to look at each other. But we cannot properly."

As for the children, they were well enough. But the eldest—"our only son, you know"—her glance became troubled. "I am so worried for him. A boy growing up in the townships . . . there are such bad influences. He needs his father's presence."

I gave her a small gift. "No. You are too kind," she said.

And, "It is so *good* to see you. Things are very difficult here now. Howu!"

She said no more of her own worries, although, under constant surveillance, she had them in plenty. Matthew had said, "A wonderful woman, Rosie. What she and Dan have sacrificed. Even now the S.B. never let her alone, they raided her house again last week."

Our encounter was too soon over, yet not soon enough. In that place our exchanges were strained. We moved toward the foyer. We shook hands. She went her separate way. I waited a few minutes before I also went out to the sunlit street.

Her presence had stirred memories. Of Dan himself, imperturbable. Of the first time I'd heard the name Dan Makhana, on New Year's Eve, when Alan had remarked, Makhana says Grobelaar looks very horrible but he's not a bad fellow. Of what Dan had said to the judge, when on trial for his life, that he and his friends had hoped by sabotage to open the ears of the Minister, because the Government had not listened during the very many years when they tried by other ways, by peaceful ways, to win their rights, ordinary human rights. Of something Matthew had told me: the first time Dan ever went to jail—for a pass laws offence—on the wall of the cell all sorts of things were scribbled, and one message moved him greatly. It said: "Oh I don't like it here I want to go home."

As I walked along the noisy pavement past shopwindows, through the press of people, I tried to imagine: Dan Makhana, now, at this moment, on Robben Island. For life.

For life without Rose. Without his children. For life. A half hour with her every three months. Supposing he lives twenty years more. Equals? . . . Christ! It equals less than two days.

I hated every individual I saw on the street. White or black, I hated them all. All of them, all of us, for allowing such a thing to happen.

"Annie, how can I possibly ask you to share my life?" We were driving slowly along a suburban road; Matthew repeatedly glanced in the rearview mirror, but now he turned to face me.

"You're not asking! It's what I want!" The thought of Rose Makhana added fury to my protest. Over lunch I'd told him of my meeting with her and it was afterward that our argument flared—I'd naturally assumed that I would live with him and he'd said this was out of the question, the S.B. watched and occasionally raided his house. "Whatever the risk," I'd cut him short, "I feel safe in your presence!" Then gently but very firmly he'd settled me and my luggage into the car.

"My dear, I can't even be frank with you, let alone honourable."

"Matthew, listen!" My command burst out as he drew up suddenly. "Look, we are living in enemy-occupied territory, we must share as much of our life as we can." I would not say, while we can.

He did not reply and I became aware of the long wait in

a street which, I saw, was empty. He realized my puzzlement and laughed.

"There now," he mocked, relieved to find a way of dissipating my intransigence, "that's what I mean. You've led a sheltered life! This for me is habit; but have you not even seen it in the cinema—the way police track a car from a distance?" I shook my head. "They have an electronic device . . . Anyway," he shrugged it off and drove on, "seems they're laying off, no sign of them since my return. They probably hope to lull."

I seized the excuse to renew my attack. "Well, then . . ."

"Here we are!" he checked me. "It's in this street," he spoke with exasperating cheerfulness, "and Shula says the flat is ideal."

He turned the car through a white gate, we were bumping down a stony red-earth track between tall pines, their trunks black from their own shade; ahead, sunlight illuminated a grove of mimosa and jacaranda.

"Ideal!" Derisively I gestured at the tangle of sere grass which surrounded us and at the crumbling colonial house.

"Come, look at the place." He took my hand to persuade me out of the car and up the steps through a front door into a hall which served three flats. He opened the door on the left and we went into large airy rooms. I had to admit they looked comfortably furnished.

"Although the rooms are big," he hastened to say, "they'll be manageable. The landlord provides a cleaner. Shula said you would want to cook?"

"At least she was right about that!" I glared at him but

it was partly in fun. I couldn't maintain my annoyance in the face of his eagerness to propitiate.

He opened a door on to the veranda and led me through. "There!"

Framed by dilapidated railings with white paint peeling, the veranda had bougainvillea and golden shower drooping from the corrugated iron roof and looked out on the ruin of a tennis court, beyond which an old eucalyptus tree reared into the blue sky, its bark wind-stripped to reveal the dazzling purity of trunk and spreading branches.

"Reconciled?"

I nodded. Already I was planning the home that could be made in this beautiful wild place. His fingers interlocked with mine and his eyes searching my face reflected the happiness that swept me; my gesture of contrition was superfluous. We sat for a time in silence on the bench which faced onto this scene. The silver-blue leaves of the eucalyptus rustled and shimmered as a breeze touched the higher branches.

When he spoke again, "My life may have to change," he said matter-of-factly. "The futile struggle in the courts— it's what they want, that we should go on playing the game their way. I feel as Kobie did . . . we who were born here, it is up to us to keep alive the spirit of revolt. Kobie . . . I wish you knew him, Annie." His face lit with the devotion he felt for his friend. "What he sacrificed . . . and if you knew how honourable a man he is, you'd understand at what cost he jumped bail . . . but to him it was unthinkable to submit to our barbaric laws." He stood up and went to the edge of the veranda where he gripped the railing and, after a moment, turned to face me. "All I can say is that I have certain responsibilities, certain tasks . . ."

"I'd like to help."

"My dear, the less you know . . . it's not for lack of trusting you, but to protect you, and others."

I stood beside him. Our bodies drew warmth from each other.

"You strengthen me, Annie."

The words sparked dread. Strengthen you for what? What was Kobie Versfeld actually doing? The police search was relentless, yet even their offer of a reward had proved fruitless.

"I didn't mean to alarm you," he smiled in self-reproach, "because we do have cause for optimism," and gaily he reminded me of the sensation of the past few weeks: journalists and former prisoners, editors and prison warders, had dared to tell the inside story of prison conditions—nothing that was not known to those who had black friends, but to the world at large the reports had come as a startling exposure—and not only had there been this brave outspokenness, but the Minister of Justice had remained abnormally mute, so that the very air we breathed seemed euphoric. "Besides"—Matthew had thought of something else—"in jail today Liberals and Communists are getting on well together . . ."

"A good theological argument," I teased, infected by his ebullience. He looked baffled. "That out of suffering comes virtue."

He laughed. "All the same, I do believe there's evidence of a new spirit, something we can build on . . . Why, Ben tells me a penal reform committee's to be set up! It's not much, I know, but it's a start!"

And perhaps, I thought, so long as hope can survive, subversion will be averted . . . Criminally optimistic, some voice echoed from the past . . .

"I'll be with you here as much as possible," he promised. "Only, tonight, would you like to stay with the Lowens? I have to be away." He would be back next morning, a Sunday, and we would have the whole day . . .

"I needn't tell you how happy Ben and I are," said Shula, as soon as she arrived at the flat to fetch me. She was studying me.

"It's all right," I said. "I know there's no question of our marrying while life is so uncertain. I'm content to wait." Content? Resigned, I should have said.

"It won't be easy," she said. "But you'll cope, hm? You've changed, you know, Cookie. You're more open, warmer— not that you weren't warm before! But it's nice, even your voice is different, rougher . . ."

"The Eastern Cape is like being in the front line of a battle," I said, and described it. Compulsively, detail after detail, I had to spell out. Everything must be told. It was absolutely essential. Quietly she listened.

Then—and it was as though I had, not resolved, but somehow been enabled to absorb and thus cope with what had been intolerable—then we busied ourselves shopping; with female pleasure we discussed and selected the requirements for life in the flat, for my life with Matthew.

In the evening, as we set out for her house, she told me their news. Jake had done well in his midyear examinations, the girls were quite manic about their dancing lessons, and in her job there'd been the thrill of the Dutch Government allocating thousands of pounds for defense of political accused. "Coming from Holland, isn't that super!" And tomorrow, she said, Ben would devote his column to prison conditions and describe what had been done in Sweden and Britain to make prisons more humane. "Perhaps, Cookie, there really will be reforms here at last!"

It was as we drew up at a traffic light that we saw a poster: *NEW DETENTION LAW.* We stopped around the corner and hurried to buy the evening paper; stood on the street corner, reading.

"Christ! They've brought back ninety days! Doubled!"

She was peering over my shoulder to see: detention in solitary confinement, without charge or trial, for up to a hundred and eighty days. Renewable! Six months of solitary confinement. Or longer. Alone in a cell. While they interrogated . . . Ostensibly so that they could question potential witnesses . . .

"Witnesses!" I cried out bitterly.

Now my fears clamoured for expression. I took Shula's arm to steer her down an empty pavement. I was sure, I said, that Matthew was involved with Kobie Versfeld . . . they must be trying to reorganize opposition, of course, but in what form, and how could they hope to keep going, let alone succeed, against such forces as the Government commanded, not to mention the informers who riddled the country. "That a man like Matthew should be driven to subterfuge and evasion!" I concluded angrily.

"There's no point in blinking the dangers," Shula said. "You know by now, Cookie, that some of us take risks for personal, for what may seem trivial, reasons. I, for instance," and she grinned, "was delighted and proud to help Kobie recently, nothing political, purely out of friendship. That's what we're reduced to, small acts for people we care about."

"Small!"

"Yes. Small. Like Ben, I have no illusions."

"And Matthew's involvement . . ."

"Goes far deeper than friendship. But you know that . . ." She looked at me in curiosity.

"Somehow it's hardly cropped up . . . he's been so busy . . ." Or had we purposely avoided the subject?

"I don't mean so much that he's a political animal, but he does have a vision of what this country could be. For that he will sacrifice himself . . . you too, I shouldn't wonder."

"You say he's not really a political animal . . ." I clutched at a phrase. Her warning struck coldly at my heart though I had to recognize its truth.

"That's not precisely what I said. But I believe his vision remains pure out of his generosity, yes, but also because he has not yet been tested by the ultimate source of corruption: by power. Paradoxical, hm?"

I could not speak for a moment. I felt closer to her than ever before even as the significance of what she'd said tormented me. Then, "Come on, it's getting late," I said. "Anyway, tomorrow Matthew will be home!"

Matthew sawed off another dead branch and tossed it on the pile he'd been building up. "What laziness," he taunted, waving the saw at me as I lay on a rug in the clearing he'd made. "And only yesterday you were so cross about your overgrown property!"

I beamed indulgently at him, relaxed, gay, on this his Sunday off. Winter would soon be over. He worked in a short-sleeved shirt; through my sweater the sun felt hot. "You've done enough," I urged, "it's lunchtime," and I went to fetch the food from the kitchen.

He opened two cans of beer, passed one to me, and I propped myself comfortably against the trunk of the old eucalyptus. He had gathered big stones, now he arranged the dry leaves and wood and prepared to light the fire. "Ages since I made a braai like this," he remarked. "I used to be rather an expert."

And were you with *her?* I couldn't check the jealous thought—his wife, divorced, in the past, why should I mind? Because she was his wife? And I, whenever the word "marriage" buzzed in my mind, swatted it like a troublesome fly. But felt an urgent curiosity, an impulse to say: tell me about her, how much did you love her, what was she like in bed, do I please you more, do you think of her still, do you love me more, *tell* me . . . "It's cold here," I said.

"Well, help me do the chops!"

While we were eating we became aware of a small black girl in a yellow dress who stood watching from under a jacaranda. The cleaner's daughter? We offered her a plate of meat and bread and butter. She took it with both hands, gravely, and a few yards from us squatted to eat. When she had finished she brought back the plate. She stood for a time looking at nothing in particular, then, abruptly, broke into a slow angular dance to some rhythm in her head, and as suddenly stopped. Again she stood staring into space.

By the time we'd finished clearing up she had gone. Matthew got up, gave a tall wide bony stretch of contentment and studied the cloudless blue sky . . . Matthew, if you know where Kobie Versfeld is . . . and without doubt a hundred and eighty days will be used on you and others to try to capture him . . . My mind swerved away, lit on a bird against the sky. "My love, is that a hawk or an eagle?" I asked, and cursed my shaky voice.

"Annie, I love you. That bird, my dear, happened to be a crow."

He settled on the rug beside me. I cushioned his head in my lap and soon he dozed. With my fingers resting in his thick hair, I wondered what it was like to be him, above all what it was like to have faith, a faith which had survived Stalin's purges . . . like a Christian's, surviving the Inquisition? . . . What a blessing that one's mind could change focus, could consign horrors to a background blur, fix sharp upon you, Matthew, and how I love you . . . and I looked upon the spare flesh stretched to the angles and hollows of the bones, the lashes resting on the faintly freckled skin, the mouth I'd once thought grim . . . and out of the images formed from the shared memories of lovers I recalled the one I liked best, of the boy—stubborn and restless he said he'd been—on the farm in the Transvaal where the wide veld throws up forested mountains, a thin wiry boy with freckled face under flaming hair, riding a horse across the veld or bicycling along the track to the store where he would buy toffees and ensnare the old Armenian who owned it into telling him for the umpteenth time stories about the Cossacks, about the Turks who had invaded Armenia, about the Caspian Sea, and about his sadly romantic emigration, while the boy himself dreamed about becoming a sailor, there was nothing he did not know about a three-masted schooner, even today he dipped into Conrad, or had, so he said, until I'd come along to disturb his peaceful nights . . . Which set me musing upon the rapturous natural connivance of our loving. . . .

He was awake, he moved to draw me down beside him so that face to face we gazed at each other, enclosed in an intimate stillness. With one hand he delineated my brows, eyes, nose, and mouth, as though to fix each feature firmly in memory. After a moment he stood up, reached down for me to follow, then hand in hand we went through the dappled sunshine of the garden into the house.

Outside our window, leaves shifted. Their shadows made patterns on the ceiling and for a moment framed his face, then sight and sound were overwhelmed by the potency of touch of taste by the ecstasy of passion shared and released until with consummation Matthew groaned, kissed me, and slept . . .

It could not have been long before I stirred, and found him awake, happy.

"I'll take you to Venice," he said. "Would you like that?"

"When shall we go?"

"One day. When it's spring . . . we'll visit the house where Tante Annetjie lived, we'll sit in St. Mark's Square, and you can ask me if the pigeons are owls or eagles."

With dignity I disentangled my legs from his. "We're *much* too bony for each other," I said.

"Oh, d'you think so? I was meditating on how extraordinarily comfortable you are."

"I, comfortable!"

"And how like Queequeg you are, Annie my dear."

"Idiot." My mouth on his silenced his retort.

Paula Waszynski 9/64
Female Prison
Bothasdorp

Dear Anne,

A 500-word jumble of thoughts! We know nothing of what's happening in the world so forgive the self-centredness.

My news is: I have a garden! Small but flourishing. Namaqualand daisies, iceland poppies just over, phlox, sweetpeas coming on. And lettuce! Enormously exciting, the anticipation of shoots, the planning of what next. Am learning the Latin names.

Thanks for Simone Weil. As you said, often incomprehensible. What's great is she barges headlong into the fact of Evil, suffering. Allows no consolations. And *if* there is a god, surely there's absolute sense in her concept: he created us by emptying the world of himself and only by emptying ourselves can he exist, functioning through us. She says every sin is an attempt to fly from emptiness, but I rushed toward emptiness—cinemas, women's magazines, thrillers—to escape the profound? To escape surrender? I like her unconventionalism, but playing rugby! Made me laugh so. And marching along in front of the workers to their acute embarrassment!

I've read that we need other people to define us. Can you imagine how one is "defined" here? Sometimes it's enough to make an undertaker laugh, sometimes in spite of all one's efforts one's soul feels like an aching tooth. And when I behave unkindly, I am oppressed at how peculiarly awful such behaviour is *here*.

But I'm learning to accept the *facts* of each day, each moment, here, to do each task as fully as possible. And what I said about Aurelius, to find freedom inside yourself. Perhaps because life is simplified one has sudden intuitions, or so it seems to me. At the oddest times! While I was scrubbing away at a hopelessly stained kitchen towel I suddenly understood something I'd read—in of all things, a science fiction novel!—The burden of Man! cried out in mockery at man, *that* burden is mine. That each of us is involved in the deeds of all men since the beginning. It is not a question of white and black or have and have not, not a question of liberal communist christian muslim hindu. It was quite clear. I am the prisoner and the jailer, the victim and the executioner. I am the jew and the nazi. They are in me and I in them by reason of our common humanity and inhumanity. Quite simply, it is a question of Man! and man. I felt exalted, I wanted at once to *live* accordingly. Of course it didn't last! Half an hour later I was the same as ever. But I do have one certainty—it's happier, nicer, to feel love than hate.

Perhaps it is in spite of ourselves that "life wins out." I wonder if you read Camus? I wonder if he and Simone Weil ever met? Yes, she was dreadfully neurotic, but what a loss if she hadn't been!

Another aim: to become like those dolls with round bottoms—Russian or Japanese?—whatever knocks you off balance you return to centre. Love to Lemkovitzes! Stay well,

Paula.

Chapter 15

*T*HE BERET WAS IN THE POCKET OF MATTHEW'S RAINCOAT —I came across it on a Monday morning as I was looking for handkerchiefs to be laundered—I'd never seen him wearing it, he disliked hats, and I knew at once he must wear it on his visits to Kobie Versfeld. Then I remembered the bulky sweater that lay on the back seat of his car although the weather was now quite warm and—in retrospect—his, "No, don't bother!" when I'd suggested packing it away, struck me as having been unnecessarily forceful.

Was this all the disguise he used? Disguise . . . When I'd read police evidence about suspects who wore dark glasses and deep-brimmed hats, or a man suddenly sporting a beard, evidence which recorded the jokes cracked by some suspects as they compared notes about their comic experiments, I'd felt the pathos of these attempts to outwit the police. Certainly Kobie Versfeld's disguise must be in a different class. That Matthew, too, should resort to these requirements of the clandestine life, came as a shock. Silly, I should have realized . . .

"Darling, is that beret all the disguise you use?" I asked

when he returned from chambers that evening. I sounded like a mother scolding her child for not wearing a vest.

He was not dismayed; he grinned. "Last Wednesday evening," he said, "on your way to dinner with Jill and Alan, you stopped at a café to buy sweets for the twins. Have you no recollection of the man who happened to pass by as you came away?"

I thought back . . . it was one of the nights when he had had to be out . . . no, I had no recollection. His expression told me it had been himself. I was fascinated but—a different shape, a different walk and posture—that was all he would divulge.

These incidentals of his secret life were in my mind as I drove, late one morning, toward the Country Club. Matthew had caught the early plane to the Eastern Cape, to argue Beatrice Qaba's appeal before the Supreme Court, while I, in bizarre contrast, was going to lunch with Sally. It was Matthew who'd clinched it. Shula, telling me Sally had telephoned and was eager to see me, mocked: "Cookie, are you going to start a straddling act again?" and indeed I was disarmed that Sally had taken the initiative; but also doubtful, until, "Shame, your cousin, after all," said Matthew.

Sally was creamily contented. "Patrick and I want you to know. I'm going to have a baby." It was easy to be pleased about that. And when we sat on the verandah surrounded by flawless lawns and gardens, it was as if nothing unpleasant had happened, either between us or anywhere else . . .

Yes. As I watched the bland faces of the golfers in their twosomes and foursomes approaching the clubhouse, and of the bridge players and other members of the club relaxed over luncheon; as I heard snatches of their conversations; it was as if nothing unpleasant was happening hundreds of miles away in the Eastern Cape or half a mile away in the pass laws court; as if there was no need for the desperate efforts of Kobie Versfeld and Matthew and those few brave enough to fight on; as if what Ben wrote about week after week was fantasy and *this*, this was the truth about the country.

Sally was telling me about the holiday they'd just had on the Continent, and in the background to her smiling face I could see an elderly African slowly sweeping the paving stones, dressed in servant's suit, white short pants with short-sleeved round-necked blouse, and wearing orange bracelets. He stopped and, leaning on his broom, bent to pick up a piece of string. Meticulously he rolled it up, tied it about, and put it in his pocket. And went on sweeping, slowly . . . I wondered how Matthew would get on; no chance of a reversal of judgment, he'd said, but a reduced sentence? And Beatrice, did she know it was today? Sally was asking the waiter about his health and his family. I had an aggravating sense of floating idly above a scene of disaster.

"And you, Anne dear, what have you been up to?"

I nearly equivocated, we'd argued so often before, but what the hell, I thought, in half an hour's time Matthew will be addressing those judges and, besides, Sally'd been sweet to the waiter. "I was down in the Eastern Cape," my voice sounded brittle, "reporting on all those trials of Africans. Especially of a teacher called Beatrice Qaba. As a matter of fact . . ."

"Yes," she said. "We read something you wrote while we were in London."

"Oh, I'm glad you saw it!" I was remembering . . . after the article had been wrung out, with its indictment of Lubbe and Mfaxa, neurotically I'd wondered: has it got through the mails? When it's published, what action will they take? Will they interrogate? . . . until there appeared in London —it was Ben who'd happened upon it low down on an inside page—an article, castrated, truncated . . . my moment of truth a damp squib. But at least Patrick and Sally had seen it!

"Yes," she said, and then it was as if a spring was released in her. "Don't you think, Anne dear, it's a bit much to write that sort of thing about your own country, a bit disloyal? Of course we all know the Nats are pretty awful, but we have to admit, don't we, that they've done a lot—all the housing—you didn't say anything about that—and the Bantustans! I mean I feel you don't even try, Anne, to see the good things. This time you've never even asked to come to my feeding scheme . . ."

She broke off to greet friends who were settling down at a nearby table. Her feeding scheme in the township—I'd gone once with her, been cheered by the sight of children benefiting from the nourishing food and her generous efficiency. Now she tipped the waiter well.

"Forgive my frankness, Anne, but you are just a mite self-righteous." She smiled to cancel out offense.

"Touché," I murmured.

Her smile softened. "Of course, *our* Bantu are streets ahead of the rest of Africa."

I'd been about to tell her, soberly, factually, about Beatrice and Mr. Qaba, and Nathaniel too, something of what their lives were, when the word "Bantu" echoed. And I remembered Beatrice, that day in the witness box, the sudden beauty of her quiet strength . . . No, I could not talk about her, not to Sally, not today, not here . . .

". . . Speakers' Corner." Sally was looking pained. "Disgusting! What black men were saying . . . vicious hatred of us! Really, you should go there when you get back . . ." She stopped and looked at me, a mite anxiously, I thought. "Of course, you *are* going back?"

"No. I am happy here."

Now she reacted to *me*, not to what I thought or believed . . . and indeed, did I not do the same with her? "I've been so selfish with our good news," she said, "but now I see, you look radiant, my dear—only much too thin —clearly you're in love . . ." She beamed. "I'm dying to know all, but I'll be patient . . . And remember, *any* time, Patrick and I would love to have you."

We parted affectionately . . . cousins, after all.

Driving away I pondered upon this division, this block, and our attempt to come to terms . . . was it not cheating to draw a line between our selves and our beliefs and actions? Yet life was full of such compromises and, at least, said an inner voice, Sally does something constructive, can see results in lives, not many but still; and what do you actually *do*? . . . No. I would never make a Marxist . . .

and I put my foot down on the accelerator and raced back toward my life with Matthew.

"My darling!" When he returned next day I held him as if he'd been away a month. "What happened?"

"Her sentence was reduced by six months."

"Is that all?"

Nearly two years of imprisonment still ahead of her . . . All the same—six months less. He'd ensured that the news was communicated to her in jail.

As for Nathaniel, he was in hiding and the police had been searching for him without success—they had raided Mr. Qaba's house on several occasions but during the past ten days had left the old man in peace. Matthew had managed to get a message to Nathaniel to say he would soon be smuggled from the country. Now we began to plan his arrival in London, who should be asked to meet him at Heathrow Airport, and where he might stay until he took up the scholarship which, so Gibbon had written, was now assured.

"But surely you must see," said Jill, "that *Who's Afraid of Virginia Woolf* is a dance of death, an allegory on the sterile nature of American society." She laughed. "I wish I could claim the idea's original!"

Nine forty-five on a Saturday night and Ben not home yet. Shula had insisted we eat. Now she said, "Well, *I* see, it's Alan who's being obtuse."

"All I say is that how ever Camus and Pinter, and all those others you talk about, darling, go on about absurdity, it was Shakespeare who had the first and last word."

" 'Life's . . . a tale told by an idiot,' " suggested Matthew. Alan grinned. " 'Signifying nothing?' " Matthew's hand held mine. "Poor Shakespeare!" His fingers played with mine . . . His small joke did not hide from me the tension he was under. When he'd come late from his chambers to fetch me and had asked if I would drive us in my car, I'd thought simply that he was exceptionally tired, but since we'd arrived—and this was an evening we'd looked forward to, it was our first opportunity to celebrate our expectations for Nathaniel—I'd realized that he was forcing gaiety.

Jake made a not unexpected appearance. "Where's Daddy?"

"Busy at the office."

"A scoop?"

"Probably. Run along or he won't tell you all about it in the morning."

"In the morning I can see all about it in the paper."

"That's not as good as Daddy telling you so don't pretend. Go along, darling."

He still hovered.

"I'll read you the Snark the next time I come." I tried bribery.

"Oh, will you? Except Uncle Matt reads it best."

I silently blessed the incorrigible child for Matthew's spontaneous laughter. "Better," I said, "not best. All right, Matt will read it next time . . ."

Jacob went, leaving us to debate the nature of the scoop —with Ben involved it must be political and we played with facetious suggestions, until, "Perhaps Johnson's called for a cease-fire?" I contributed. "Or," this from Matthew, "Smith's declared independence at last." Which brought scorn from Shula who quoted Ben's, "That upstart would never dare cock a snook at Wilson and the West!"

"A scoop?" It was Jill who first noticed Ben's sudden arrival.

"A scoop all right!" he exclaimed, kissing Shula briefly. "S.B. raid on our offices! Everyone searched! Passports seized! Tonight! Silly buggers couldn't have timed it better to catch our Sunday headlines!"

Shock at the news and amusement at the crass stupidity rippled through us; then: "Your passport, Ben?" Shula's question, spoken with cool casualness, chilled the electric atmosphere.

"Yup. I joined you, Matt, as one of the honoured band of citizens the Government can't bear to part with. *And* the bastards swiped my prison reform material. "

Matthew offered a cigarette to Shula. She was about to accept with a grateful glance, her hand shaking slightly as it reached out, when she realized Ben was helping himself to a stiff whisky. Her hand dropped.

"Is it that bad, Ben?" Matthew asked.

There was an uncomfortable silence which stretched on as Ben, glass in hand, came toward us at the table. I had a nightmare fear that he might chuck the whisky in Matthew's face; then he began to smile, very sweetly, and leaned across the table to pour it into the vase of flowers in the center.

"Always make sure the receptacle has a bottom to it," he said. "I once poured a sickeningly sticky raspberry drink into one of those shell-case vases—First World War vintage—and it came straight through and down the back of a lady's neck. Let that be a lesson to you, Matt, you old bugger, you."

Jake was back. "Jacob!" Shula shrieked at him. All her anxious misery concentrated in anger against what was dearest to her. "*Will* you go!"

Jake hid his fright by making Chinese faces at her.

"It's all right, Shula my treasure, it's all right." Ben ruffled Jake's hair and gave him a gentle shove toward the door. "O.K., Jake son, I'll come up to you in a minute."

He accompanied Jake out. The telephone was ringing. We could hear his exaggerated groan as he went to answer.

Matthew lit a cigarette. Alan cleared his throat. Shula was crumbling bread as the slow seconds passed.

Ben was back. "They've arrested the lot! All the warders and ex-prisoners who gave affidavits! They're to be charged with giving false information to the press. And Mendelbaum is to prosecute!"

Mendelbaum. An Orthodox Jew. Notorious.

Jill spoke, "I hope to God Paula doesn't get to hear that."

Alan said, "I'll find some excuse to see her on Monday."

Shula tidied the bread she'd crumbled. "I expect it'll be our prisoners' defence fund next," she said.

Matthew turned to Ben as he sat down and began to eat his dinner. "Would you like to discuss the legal aspects, for what that's worth?" He was smiling but, watching him, I'd seen hope demolished.

"Thanks, but why waste time?" said Ben . . .

We left soon after. Matthew drove—far too slowly, I

thought. I felt the flat was a safe haven against the ominous forces that gathered and longed to get back.

After we'd talked again about the arrests, what, I asked, had troubled him earlier. "I mean even before Ben got back?"

"Nothing serious . . . they've begun tailing me again, pretty consistently."

"What busy bees they are all of a sudden." I was determined not to sound anxious.

"A full-time job, their business."

"Darling, what a bore for you!"

"Mind if I stop for cigarettes," he asked, but it was a formality. Already he was drawing up at a café and "Of course not," I said, then waited, chafing at the delay.

When he returned to the car I watched as he lit a cigarette before driving on. "Come on," I urged, "you've not told me everything."

He had to brake for a traffic light.

"After tonight, Annie, I must not stay in the flat."

"Don't be ridiculous!"

"My dear, I've given way to my feelings, selfishly risked your safety . . ."

"No, no!" Angrily I insisted, "I'm in this with you. If . . ." I was about to say, If we were married there'd be no question . . . "There must be something I can do!"

"The less you know . . ."

"For God's sake, Matthew! You go on as if you're planning sabotage!" By taunting I hoped to discover the level of the danger he faced.

"No, that's long past." His quiet statement only exasperated me.

We'd reached home. He slowed down for the white gate. Moonlight splotched the earth. As the car bumped along the track through the pine trees I tackled the thought: guerrilla action, then. At last I rounded on him. "Madness!" But I kept my voice low. "When people get arrested simply for writing a few articles, you're crazy to take such risks!"

Ah, now he reacted! In the moonlight I glimpsed his face, stern, before he parked in dark shadow, then he shook his head. "You draw a curious conclusion, my dear. You regard it as more sensible, then, to invite drastic punishment for what would amount to piecemeal reforms?"

He spoke with a bitterness so uncharacteristic that it drove me to a furious sarcasm: "But you, you were excited about the prison reform committee!"

"I was wrong to indulge in such optimism . . . to forget for one moment the futility of muddling along on vague liberal premises."

"You treat me like a child!"

"No, Annie, never that, you're everything to me. But there are others to consider . . . Why am I telling you . . . you know . . ."

"You believe people are perfectible!" My voice broke out of the low-pitched exchanges and with shrill emphasis I continued—I had lost track of the relevance—"You believe you can transform society! Just how do you transform man's nature!" I wanted to throw open the door, smash the mood, but was held by some compulsion. I felt intolerably alone. Nor did he move. We sat cooped up, hostile. Until I could contain it no longer. "What the hell does Versfeld think he's doing? There are too many rotting in jail; Christ, what for?" I hurled the words at the windshield. "Matthew, I want to go . . . before it's too late!"

His silence was unrelenting. But when, finally, I dared to glance at his face I saw there a sadness that was unbearable. My hand closed over his, fiercely he returned the pressure, then he sprang from the car and opened my door. All the anger spilled away. He held me, in the stillness. It's all right. It's got to be all right.

Then passionately he thrust me from him, his hands gripped my wrists as he confronted me, against his anguish the pain he caused came as a relief. "You want to go! Annie, you really want to go?" His hold relaxed, remorsefully he kissed my wrists and said slowly, "But I would not try to dissuade you."

I was shaking my head and smiling. "No, my love, no, that's not what I meant!" The misunderstanding seemed so ludicrous, it canceled out the earlier conflict. "How could you imagine? I wouldn't dream of going without you." I was kissing his face, his hands, and laughing softly, until he, at last convinced, sighed and smiled.

The moonlight glowed on the path through the high grass. With his arm tight about my shoulders, we walked silently toward the house, and up the steps to the veranda. Finally he spoke, "I can't bear to see you hurt, but my dear, you must understand I have commitments, you yourself have talked of being committed."

"It's committal to you I meant, to life!"

"I am nothing. We are nothing. This insistence on the personal, the individual!" Ruefully he turned from me to open the veranda door. Then abruptly he closed it again and led me back into the garden. Under a clear patch of sky we stopped.

"I cannot talk to you about my friend," he said, his voice low, "but you should know that there is not any question of guerrilla action, it would be—as you remarked—madness now. But in time, who knows? Meanwhile we must prepare, organize, train . . . men and women must be equipped, I don't mean only for war but for peace. It is not easy . . . there are those in exile who want action now, regardless of the readiness of the people here . . ."

"But that's idiotic! I mean it's so obvious. But they *must* listen to you, you're here, you know!" I too, spoke softly.

He shook his head. "They live in another world. They argue that we have the wrong perspective, we are too close to the scene!" He smiled at the irony of it. "Besides, they're under continual pressure from African states . . . But, Annie, there are unknown factors—Rhodesia, and Portugal too—can Salazar's successor keep the iron grip over Angola and Mozambique?"

"Oh, Matthew, yes! Of course, that would be the turning point!"

"In the long run we shall win. And we have to stay in our own country, we need something to build on, *here*."

Our own country . . . above us the moon floated serenely in the clear patch of sky. The trunk of the old tree shone whitely for a time before the earth turned and the moonlight slid on. "Funny," I said, "I get no feel of Africa down here in the South."

"Nonsense! Feel it!" His hands spread out as if they could touch the air, hold and offer it to me, too, to touch, and for the first time I felt—as in Kenya or Rhodesia—something potent, to do with tall grass and low trees near the surface of the earth, the vastness of the night with its silence and its noises—yes, this is Africa!

In bed we held each other fiercely. Desperately we tried to arouse each other but our mouths proved numb, our sex dry within us. What had been natural was now complicated . . . In the end I moaned and shuddered as if my climax had come and lay, a cheat, feeling all bones and damp skin, terribly confronted by loneliness. After a while he, then I, got up and washed—the act of love had become an indecorous performance. I went to the kitchen, to return after a while with glasses of hot milk. After we had drunk it he folded me in his arms and said, "Annie, what we have is so precious nothing can harm it. Nothing!" I cushioned his head against my breasts, and watched until he slept . . .

Early on Sunday morning I helped him pack—everything of his, there must be no trace. And as he took his toothbrush from the mug it had shared with mine I saw the fragile domesticity we had created disintegrate before my eyes.

Outside, he piled the suitcases into the trunk of his car. A bird started up, like a dentist's drill, shrill.

"Annie, I promise to take care."

"That damn bird! It's got such a menacing thing."

He laughed. "It's got something to shout about. Look!"

He aimed a pebble to one side of its din. There was a flash of scarlet and yellow and black.

His hand drew my hair back from my face, gave it a gently reproachful tug. I smiled, then his mouth was on mine, his body crushed mine to his, and what a few short hours before had been arid now melted and surged and sprang in me . . . but he had gone, he waved as the car moved off through the trees, I was standing alone, while the longing throbbed in me more excruciatingly than I yet had known it, the longing to bear his child.

Chapter 16

N͟O NEED TO CONSULT MY WATCH TO KNOW IT WAS NEAR one o'clock—the tables in Chez Bertrand were always punctually filled. In the mounting buzz of voices as waiters and lunchers greeted, consulted, discussed, I watched for Matthew from a quiet corner table . . . our first date since he'd moved from the flat. I could hardly keep from laughing, so vibrant was my expectation, and I tried to think seriously about my activity of the morning—in the library, I'd searched through photographs of the city when it had been little more than a mining camp—I was writing an article on the few old buildings, the rare arcade that survived. Now, as I stared at the heavy traffic in the street where sunlight was blocked out by the high buildings, I could visualize, as in a double exposure of a photograph, the dorp of seventy years ago, with occasional carts and horses on its wide dusty roads, roads which meandered between rough wooden buildings roofed with corrugated iron. All at once, because of Matthew, the city was invested with glamor . . . again laughter surfaced. Besides, it was one o'clock, the restaurant conveniently near to his chambers . . . I glanced at the menu—trout, perhaps?

"Why Anne, good to see you!" Walt Tree stood beside the table; with him was Helen Mills. They cut short the pleasantries and simultaneously, their faces and voices agitated, asked: "Have you heard? The first one hundred and eighty day arrest!" And, "A friend of Kobie Versfeld's," Helen added.

"Oh God, no! Who?"

It was not Matthew. I did not know the man. Poor thing . . . poor wretched man . . . The first one hundred and eighty day arrest.

The headwaiter approached me with a letter; a messenger had delivered it, he said. It was a short, careful note, written, apparently, two hours earlier: "Forgive me. I do not know where to find you this morning and I have to leave immediately, see some people in the country, probably only a week or two. It is better that I do not write. Take care."

Out of politeness I asked Helen and Walt to join me; then, with them, ordered something and tried to eat. From an adjacent table came men's voices: ". . . that chap detained, obviously, a Communist . . . " "Well, I've no sympathy, after all, it goes on all the time in Russia . . ." "True enough . . ."

A waiter was protesting at how little I'd eaten; I pretended illness and hurriedly left. When I reached home I walked through the coarse grass and stood gazing at the overgrown tennis court. Sunshine filled the garden. There was a stirring of leaves and birds and insects . . . a vague hum of traffic . . . what was it Keith Gibbon had said . . . the professionals were all on the other side . . . there was absolutely no possibility of organizing a popular movement, not under such a tyranny . . . One of my neighbours drove up, called out in greeting, I waved back and saw beyond her the flash of a bird's flight against the dark pines—yellow and scarlet and black—I escaped inside where I began to sort the notes I'd made that morning on the mining dorp of seventy years ago.

Each day I searched through the newspapers and endured the vulgar propaganda of the radio in case something had happened to Matthew . . . not that it would necessarily be reported—they took care to keep us guessing. The next victim they hauled into the hundred and eighty day net was a woman, who remained anonymous for some while; then, so we gathered, it was more than likely she was a friend of Kobie Versfeld's. Yes, rumour was confirmed, an old political friend. Next a man was taken in, an African, and there were rumours of others. Advocates resorted to *habeas corpus* and hope sprang . . . But a new law was rushed through, just as there could always be a presidential proclamation, and the loophole was quickly sealed. Just as any party or organization could be outlawed at the stroke of the Minister's pen, and the latest to be knocked off was—as Shula had feared—the fund for the defence of political prisoners. Meanwhile, in suburbs throughout the city, at dawn eight hundred or a thousand police raided servants' quarters, to net eight hundred, a thousand, two thousand, men and women and teen-agers, alleged to be illegally there. No matter that they might be husbands, wives, children, or simply lovers . . . only the servant was "legal." With the courts already overflowing, trials were held in the police cells.

For everyone else life went on much as usual. In the northern suburbs householders told gardeners to fill the swimming pools; spring had come. Theatre critics agreed on the excellence of a local production of Brecht's *Caucasian Chalk Circle*, and Marlene Dietrich won nightly ovations at the Civic Center when she sang "Where Have All the Flowers Gone?" to the white middle class of the city . . . Shula drove the children to and from school and to their art and dancing classes. I worked on the survey and mailed a new installment overseas. Jill was more than usually restless because Alan was away in the Eastern Cape, defending ten bus drivers accused of furthering the aims of communism . . .

"Alan, wonderful to see you! When did you get back?"

"This morning. Anne . . ."

"You're just in time for tea."

"Not now, but thanks. Anne . . . Nathaniel Qaba has been taken. A hundred and eighty days."

Nathaniel . . . "Oh no!" After a moment—"When?" I wanted to know.

"About three weeks ago."

Three weeks. Matthew had been gone twenty days.

Alan was saying, "Oliver Woolley only just heard. Nathaniel had been in hiding, perhaps you knew. Apparently he could no longer stand the uncertainty and went one night to the township. The police picked him up in his cousin's house."

The fool, the bloody, bloody fool.

"Yes?" I urged. "You must know more?"

Reluctantly he related what Nathaniel's cousin had told Oliver . . . how they had come at two in the morning, bursting in in their usual way, and dragged Nathaniel from bed, in front of all the children . . . how they hadn't let him dress, forced him away in his underwear . . . how the sergeant kicked him through the doorway . . . the kids were screaming . . . and Nathaniel nearly unconscious by the time they got him to their truck.

Nathaniel.

"Anne. He's agreed—if you can put it that way—to become a State witness."

Nathaniel. The name sighed through me in lamentation . . . Eventually I said, "If only Beatrice doesn't get to know."

And Mr. Qaba . . . I was clutching at myself, groping in terrible isolation after Matthew . . . from whom no word had come since those few lines in the restaurant.

"Alan"—the question had been hammering at me and must be answered; I heard my voice calm, careful—"you think Matthew might be taken at any time?"

His hand gripped my shoulder, in warning rather than reassurance. I looked up into his face. He nodded. As if I did not know! Yet it rocked me.

"Why does he do it? I mean what the hell for? What do they think they're up to? How could they allow Nathaniel to be taken?" My disloyalty to Matthew ached. "There's too many rotting in jail. And all the time that creature Vorster . . . Lubbe, the lot of them, just crushing everybody, their minds, their souls!"

Alan's arms came round me as I sobbed and he held me tight until I'd cried myself dry. He mopped at my tears with his handkerchief.

"Listen," he said, "you're to come to Helen's party. We'll fetch you."

I shook my head, and in the end persuaded him I was fine, all I needed was an early night, a long sleep.

After he'd gone I took the tea out to the veranda, drank thirstily, and fought fear with rigid concentration on what my eyes could see . . . the eucalyptus with its silver-blue leaves shimmering . . . there must be a breeze. The first breath of wind bringing rain to break the drought? Matthew could surely have found some way to send a message. A cloud had appeared, the size of a man's hand, it was growing . . . now reared itself into a giant shape . . . now glided away, its burden of moisture intact. His gay hopefulness, that first time we'd looked out on the wild garden. The optimism—pathetic—of farmers and tribesmen, day after day, their gaze raking the sky, their ears alert, any faint shift of air and they'd believe it to be an intimation. Nearly three weeks since he'd left. And in the weeks to come the wind would grow warmer, to carry famine, death, in its parched breath as the drought dragged on year after year after year.

Sharp reports banged out. A continual rat-a-tat-tat; Stengun practice at the local police station. Rifle fire too, ex-

ploding against the crescendo of the Sten guns . . .
Against such power what hope was there of the people
here ever being ready . . . optimism—pathetic—criminal
. . . Over the rim of the teacup I glimpsed, at the borders
of the garden, a movement, and focused on the broken-
down fence where a frieze of black men in romper suits
threaded their way through the bushes, a leisurely trail of
servants from neighbouring apartment houses going dead
happy to their Saturday afternoon pastime, to their illegal
boozing, their shebeen in the woods, against the rat-a-tat-tat
of neighbouring police gunmen at their Saturday pastime . . .

Matthew . . . where? What doing? Who with? Jealousy sprang. Jealous! Yes. Because your moments hours
days weeks, your smile, your words and silences, your risks,
are shared with others. Jealous of those others, whoever,
wherever . . . I fought back with memories . . . and,
Matthew, I love you! Then terror revived . . . Nathaniel
—interrogated—could he, might he, betray Matthew?

I fled from myself and my fears—"I've changed my
mind," I told Alan when I telephoned, "idiotic to sit about."
And sought refuge that night among the huddle of people
at Helen's party. The room was thick with bodies and
smoke and noise. In the half-dark, and with a second drink
bringing no relief, I wished I had not come. Perhaps to an
outsider it looked like a good party. But could there be any
escape? From the thought of Nathaniel—being interrogated,
now? From the knowledge of Beatrice in jail, *now,* and
Makhana, Mandela, all the others, locked in their cells on
the Island, *now,* while Rose and the wives were thrust away

in the townships, *now*. Through an archway in the next room, I could see people dancing to a Louis Armstrong record . . . that woman, laughing as she does the twist, must be thinking, my husband is in Pretoria jail, *now*, and the girl dancing with a student who once was in ninety days, her father is in one hundred and eighty days, *now*. And you, Matthew, my love, are where, *now?* . . . Shockingly sorrow turned to frantic furious resentment—against Versfeld, against the Party, against Matthew!

"Ben, love, pour me a drink," I appealed.

Ben dutifully concluded the stroke-by-stroke demonstration of cricket he'd been giving for Sven Björnstrand, a Swedish consul. Jill was caught up in animated conversation with a poet. Shula looked sleepy. Alan was talking intently to a British diplomat and his wife, a blonde in strawberry pink. Ben and the Swede drifted over to them and were soon—heads together—deep in the discussion . . . With a flourish of Satchmo's trumpet the record came to an end. There was a slow fading of voices, then silence. Which was penetrated by a voice, loud, empty: "Really, you people are most extraordinary!" Each syllable rang out. It was the blonde in strawberry pink. "All you talk about is people in prison or on trial. Really, it is most *peculiar!*" Blinking slightly, she looked around.

The Beatles blared forth. Helen refilled my glass. "Do rescue Walt," she said. We could hear him talking to a French journalist. Suddenly the Frenchman was berating him: "I was in Hanoi! There's nothing you can tell me!" While Walt, with flushed dignity, protested, "It's not that simple you know." "Walt!" I called. "Come and dance."

Eagerly he turned to me, and we joined the crowd dancing in the dimness . . . "Summertime," with the lazy grunts of a saxophone . . . "You've a neat sense of rhythm," he commented. "Americans dance marvellously," I said, thinking—you don't dance, Matthew, at all. You're too serious, too damn dedicated.

"Haven't seen Matthew of late, what's he up to?" Walt's innocent question struck home.

"Away on some case," I fumbled with falsity, angry that Matthew had put me in this position. Before Walt could pursue his interest, "Go rescue Helen," I urged, "she's being polite to someone." He went along happily.

Alan was dancing with Jill, the poet cut in, Alan strolled off in search of a drink, I made after him. He greeted me with, "Hey, I'm high." I peered at him. "Why, so you are! Good for you! I thought you were perfect . . . perfectible! Never mind, so am I!" "What, perfect?" "No, no, high, can't you tell?"

At some point he said, "Time to go. Jill's signalling she's had enough."

"I'll drive," said Jill, firmly.

She drove, Alan with his long legs stretched out beside her, I in the back. They bickered about the poet. She said how charming he was. "Hell, Jill, but obviously queer." "Well, my angel, that can be extremely cozy. He knows Paris well, and Athens, he has very wide interests." "You mean not just law?" "I mean he's not buried in cases fourteen hours a day, he sees there's something else in life—theater, art." "And music too, I've no doubt!" "You're so right! *And*," she tossed it at him, "he's extremely articulate." "Everything seems to be extreme with you tonight, Jill." "Yes, including the extreme inebriation of my husband." "Oh, come on . . ." "Anyway, I don't believe he's queer, only aloof . . ."

My longing for Matthew gnawed incessantly. Quickly I opened the window. And with the intrusion of the cold night came clear rational thought. Matthew's words: "I am nothing. We are nothing. This insistence on the personal, the individual!"—I'd thought them rueful, now their significance devastated . . . and Shula's, ". . . He will sacrifice himself . . . you too . . ." Matthew endangered, and I, cast off, abandoned.

Ahead of us, suddenly, something cluttered the street, remains of an accident. A handful of people in the uncertain light clustered around a body, lying there.

As we drove by, "Looks like an African," said Jill.

"Mm," grunted Alan. "And if I am drunk, why shouldn't I be?"

I felt at screaming pitch . . . Of course an African! Bodies, in the road like that, are. Anonymous. Alan, make us stop! Do something! . . . He'd lapsed into silence . . . Alan, you bloody hypocrite! I felt betrayed, demented. Matthew! I want to break—no, Alan I mean, I want to break you punish you!

"Jill! I want to go to my cousin's, please could you drop me there?" Busily I began to repair my makeup. "These new streetlights make one look a fright."

In the driveway of Patrick's house I got out of the car, thanked them hurriedly, and started toward the front door. All at once my head was swimming, nausea rippled through me, became a shudder, my stomach began to heave, I felt everything must spew out, the appalling mess of drink and jealousy and anguish of hatred frustration love terror . . . the body . . . dood tevrede . . . the Qabas and all the others . . . dood tevrede and my body retching so that I steadied myself against a tree trunk and leaned over, one hand fastidiously holding back my dress while from my mouth spurted a brief sour trickle which I patted away with my handkerchief, thinking how much nicer a handkerchief is than a Kleenex and how lucky that I'm here in my own country where there is a dead happy black woman to wash and iron away all traces of my vomit and snot. I was shivering . . . I ran toward the side door and entered . . . inside it felt warm and safe. I slipped upstairs to a bathroom, threw away the sodden handkerchief, was violently sick, rinsed my mouth out, sat for a while, put lipstick on, stood shakily to check in the mirror on what I looked like and encountered glittering eyes . . . I felt frighteningly alive . . .

I came down to a brightly lit formal party, with Patrick approaching me, a glass of champagne held out, to kiss me and say, "Anne dear, how nice that you've come. My, you look beautiful." He began to laugh. "D'you know, I'm reminded of the time Lance dared you to put some unspeakable insect in your mouth. You were very frightened—white with fear—but you did it! Then, afterward, can you remember, you were so surprised to find you were still alive. You went quite wild!"

Sally was kissing my cheek. "Super you made it!" She pulled back to observe me. "No, Patrick my sweet, champagne is *not* what she needs; cosset her and introduce her to some nice people!"

Obediently I went with him.

"Anne Dawson! Where have you been all this time?" Henry Thomson stood beside me. His amused glance sharpened as he regarded me, but his manner was concerned. "Patrick, I'll take care of her."

I felt suspicion and animosity give way to defiance.

"Come, sit over here." With kind quiet words he reassured. "Let me get you a brandy, you're so pale."

The brandy established comfort and warmth.

"It's the unspeakable insect," I said.

He settled in a chair facing me. "Tell me about the unspeakable insect." His attentiveness—so I persuaded myself—was that of one watching a chameleon to catch it in the act of changing color.

"No," I said—now what was it I felt? Disarmed? Triumphant?—"You tell me about all these unspeakable people."

"Ah. I thought those green eyes of yours had a wicked sparkle. All right, you asked for it!" Mockingly he complied, and soon I was laughing at his caricatures of the people around us who talked about golf and polo and stocks and shares and weekends at White River. I was laughing a lot.

"There. You had me scared," he said. "But even when you're deathly pale you look ravishing."

He took me by the hand, led me to the veranda where people were dancing. He drew me to him, held me steadily still for a moment . . . My God, what's come over me, I thought, then we were moving with the music . . .

He was driving me home. The car jogged and jostled us as he took the rough drive too fast. We reached the house. He switched off the engine, the lights, he was kissing me, wilfully my dry lips parted, I gasped with the violence of the wild urge that possessed me, his hands were on me, wave after wave rose in my flesh until my craving became torment.

"Anne!"

We went in. I led him quickly to the spare room. Then we were mouths gorging each other's kisses, bodies grappling in the dark, he with a need for four-letter words as he thrust furious fast till his plunges of lust turned words to a sob of release. And I—high and dry I dimly thought, meaning to escape through levity and, stop now! I told myself, at least save that—"Oh Henry quick!" I beseeched. He had only to touch and the great wave poised in terrible suspense pounded against the hold of his hand. And was over.

When he had gone, I lay there.

A void . . . an eternity it seemed in that dark room, dark all around and within . . . And in that inner dark a faint voice moaning, what have I done? what have I done? over and over and over . . .

Until horror filled the void, and sour loathing of myself. I made as if to tear my hair but there was no escape in gestures, in thoughts, in tears. There was nothing . . . Nothing.

Late in the morning Alan telephoned. "Come and sober up with some spring planting," he said. "Jill and I are full of good earthy intentions." Impossible to tell what he'd sensed. What did it matter? I had destroyed everything that mattered.

We spent the day pottering in the garden, seldom talking unless to the twins, who contrived to lose the trowels and forks in a surprising variety of places. I was dazed, belaboured by dull hatred of myself and the knowledge that nothing I could ever do, *ever*, would undo my act. I must not, I dared not, think of Matthew. And how . . . why? I asked myself. Dear God, how could I . . . ? What am I that I could not only destroy such perfect happiness but that I . . . that cheap and barbarous . . . Vengeance? Because Matthew valued something more than our happiness? No . . . there was no escape through questioning . . . no exoneration . . . My hands trembled as they placed a plant into the groove I had scooped out, and pressed it down into the cool soil.

At sunset, as we collected our tools and moved toward the house with Mike and Lucy tagging along, Alan remarked quietly, inconsequentially, "Nothing much matters really. Which is precisely what matters." A church bell was tolling faintly, it must be a long way off. "To put defeat into one's personal equation . . ." he went on, "it's a beginning." What he said, the vacuum in which he said it in an offhand way, was so curious that neither Jill nor I appeared to react. The phrases hung in the air, in our lives . . .

Matthew had been gone twenty-seven days. It was a morning of clouds and bitter cold, a sudden reversion to winter long past, there must be snow on the Berg. It was a midday of clear skies and brilliant sun, and on the strong wind which swept the clouds from the heavens came a host of butterflies. Yellow and white they fluttered everywhere. I watched them from my window as they flickered against the dark green of the pines. It's no good, I was thinking, when down the drive bumped a car. So it became the day of Matthew's return.

He was there, before my eyes, safe. I was holding him, safe . . .

After a time, "Annie, come to the coast for a few days," he said.

Chapter 17

*O*UTSIDE THE CINEMA IN THE GLARE OF LIGHT PEOPLE jostled me. I should have been moving with the throng toward the parking lot but I stood, waiting. Would Matthew make it? I willed, I prayed that he would. We'd calculated exactly, intending him to draw up at the curb as the bulge of the audience spilled from the doors. He'd told me the model and colour of the car he was hiring. No sign yet . . .

"Annie, come to the coast for a few days," he had said. And left unspoken the reason for this urgent retreat. Of his tour he'd said little . . . but clearly there had been disappointment. Of Nathaniel's tragic capture he had said that two days before he was due to see Nathaniel with instructions for the journey north, Nathaniel had made the disastrous visit to the township. Would I ever know more? Did I want to? Better not. Safer for Matthew and for myself. Good that, positive, to think in terms of safety rather than danger. And so I'd asked no questions, welcomed this departure for the coast as a reprieve from what I dreaded, his insight into my grubby betrayal . . .

The crowd was thinning. If he didn't arrive it meant

he'd failed to throw off the men who had been tailing him on and off for weeks, in one place or another—that much I knew. Determinedly I pushed panic to the back of my mind, only to recall the moment earlier in the day when, "Dearest, you look exhausted," I'd said, and held him tight. He was back! Safe! Held him for a long while for the blessed feel of his body, yes, but also to escape his loving gaze.

The commissionaire was closing the doors. The flow of cars had almost ceased. I was conspicuous, a woman alone late at night in the empty street.

A gray Ford. Thank God! And no car within sight behind it. It drew up. Matthew leaned across to open the door. His face was pale, dreadfully tired, full of concern— "I *am* sorry to be late."

"I never thought I'd make it," he said, as we drove off.

"Were they on to you?"

"With luck, they're still sitting outside a restaurant in Hillbrow."

When we were securely out of town and on the main road to the southeast I insisted on driving. A measure of his fatigue that he did not argue, and soon I sensed a lessening of tension until his body slackened in sleep, his head rested against my shoulder.

Perhaps, I was thinking, perhaps I can learn to live with the truth as part of my daily burden. Was that what Alan had meant—to put defeat into one's personal equation— but precisely how? Nathaniel, are you in Rooihell? Or free and guilt-burdened, suffering the contempt of friends, the contempt of Mfaxa. I remember your voice, scathing, "Impimpis!" Nathaniel, how do you live with it? Yet here I am, living . . . I looked down at Matthew's face, vulnerable in sleep. His eyelids flickered, were still once more. Suddenly a rabbit darted into the road ahead and was transfixed by the headlights. I stopped just in time. It crouched, paralyzed; when I turned the lights off it sprang away in the veld.

Matthew had awakened.

"Oh darling," I said, "what have I done?" I hardly knew what I was saying.

His expression was grave. "Annie," his voice was oddly dull, "I've taken so much for granted. I've been dishonest. Never spoken of the future, hardly spoken of loving you. I've no right to do so now . . ." He stopped short and tried again, dry and low. "All I'm trying to say is, I am deeply conscious . . ."

I silenced him, "Please don't!" I plunged. "Don't ever talk of your being dishonest, it's me that's . . ."

"Standerton!" he exclaimed, his hand over mine on the wheel to slow me down.

Standerton. We drove along a main street of cold lights, of bald shops and offices and gas stations ugly in the pre-dawn desolate landscape. Standerton. Gratefully I considered its sudden appearance . . .

We went on steadily to the southeast, through infinitely creased hills and valleys, through miles and miles of pale green-plush sugar plantations until, late in the afternoon, we reached the small village where Jill owned a place near the sea. Following the instructions on the map she had drawn, we came upon the cottage, white thatched rondavels which linked to form several rooms. Too tired to look around or to eat, we had a bowl of soup, and, casually, I suggested, "Why not use the single beds tonight? We're both worn out." As though to preserve him from corruption.

I woke to blazing sunlight and quietness. Matthew was still sleeping. A quick shower and I pulled on my bathing suit and a terry cloth robe. While I made coffee I looked about the living room. The canvas chairs, scrubbed wood tables, the heavy woven mats, everything was bleached and peaceful. I became aware of the mug I was holding, its grainy texture, and under my bare feet the rough reed of the matting. I wondered whether to wake him. He slept with only the sheet rumpled over his body. He stirred sleepily, rubbed his eyes, and was instantly wide awake.

"You look miles better," I said.

He stretched hugely, yawned, and breathed deep. "The sea air!" he exclaimed, and, "Good morning, Annie," he pulled me toward him for a kiss. "Breakfast!" I announced and hurried to check on the coffee and eggs.

Then out into the brilliant moist warmth of a tropical spring morning, small lizards darting as we moved along the sandy track through the jungle which rimmed the land, past wild palms, tatter-leafed bananas, guava and pawpaw. Looking and laughing and starting to trot; there, beyond the dunes, sparkled the Indian Ocean. Above us two gulls flirted in flight as we passed through the succulent green carpet clinging to the dunes, on to the sand, cool and firm from the night's dew. The only other footprints, the gulls'. Laughter was fixed on our faces by the salt breeze and the dazzling light.

"Race you!" I said and tore into the frothing shallows. Matthew passed me and forged ahead, swimming with confident strokes, diving under breakers until he was far out, bobbing, waving, calculating the approaching swells. I felt a twinge of anxiety, wished the beach were not so empty, only some kids turning cartwheels, then saw him select a massive swell and, as its crest lifted and began to curl forward, throw himself with it, catching the downward plunge and riding its foamy force on and on till he lay on his stomach in the shallows.

"You're a marvel!" I called out.

"Come, let me show you," he said. He looked ten years younger. He took my hand and I let myself go with him toward the deep waters, but though I flung my body forward as the wave surged, after a few yards I sagged and was left behind. "Elan but no follow through," was his opinion.

I made for shallower water and floated, luxuriating in the thought of his prowess. I stood to watch him again. A huge breaker was almost on me. I dived. Too late. I was hurled under, whirled and thumped into a somersault, my brain and limbs whipped in turmoil. I fought for control, gulped seawater, and was savagely tossed again. With breath gone, a drumming in my head, darkness endless darkness terror mortality striking . . .

Hands had hold of me. A convulsion of relief. Air and light and a glimpse of Matthew's face, concerned, amused, teasing. "Like your politics. Your dive. All heart and guts."

Aggression sparked and subsided. I was powerless to speak. I drifted, listless, vulnerable, to the sea, to life, to my weakness, my sin . . . the hands tightened their hold. I looked up at him. Tears of humiliation blurred my vision. He shook me tenderly. In the candour of his gaze, I was exposed. I could not tell what he saw or sensed, nor—it suddenly became apparent—did it matter. Irresistibly I was open to him. The woman, flawed, vain, shameful, myself, whom Matthew loved. His hands gripped my shoulders, drawing me to him, his mouth on mine tasted of salt. It was a brief statement of love.

Other bathers were approaching the shallows. We waded out and, hand in hand, at a measured trot, headed home.

There, screened by the dark-leafed thorny matingulu hedge, on the grass outside the cottage we made love. It was as if he thoughtfully, sweetly, restored and redeemed me so that I was freed . . . perhaps the properties of earth and sky combined with his probity—ah, why try to define what was for me, purely and simply, a miracle. Purely . . . yes, it was like the first time, a discovering, until we affirmed each other and a sort of gaiety took possession of us until our pounding hearts signalled sexuality pure and simple. Until emptied, fulfilled, we lay in a dark languor on the grass under the sun and he said dreamily, "You can almost feel the pulse of the earth."

The days took on their rhythm. We bathed. We fished, idly, not from the beach, which by afternoon was too crowded, but along the white sands to the south. The withdrawal of waves, the undertow, would pull the line so that we braced ourselves and felt all the fine expectancy of a catch, sometimes to find there was indeed a fish to be tugged in, to be cleaned and cooked and consumed. Some evenings he worked on legal briefs he had brought while I read, others, we played cards. Occasionally heavy flying beetles attracted by the lamps clicked their way through the still air. If the electricity faltered we moved out from the veranda and sat under the stars. The Southern Cross acquired significance. We hardly talked. Actions, emotions seemed elemental, sufficient in themselves, as if we no longer had the enclosing shell of our skin and flesh but our lives flowed together. Before bed we walked along the sands and heard the chatter of monkeys in the jungle undergrowth. Approaching the lagoon to the north we could smell the putrid sweetness from the sugar mill, hear from all sides the liquid notes of small frogs.

There were rock pools to crouch over, miniature underwater worlds of shells, anemones, seaweed, tiny fish and crabs; we stared by the hour.

I came upon an exquisite shell, showed it to him. "See? Even this tiny hole in it is perfect."

He studied it. "That tiny hole, Annie my dear, was bored by the predator in order to kill off the creature inhabiting the shell."

"Oh." Indecent that destruction, death, could have any perfection . . . although—the end result of every living thing being death—you become "perfectly" dead . . . I was about to utter this original proposition when the truth of it hit me: Matthew, you, perfectly dead, Matthew, you, perfectly dead! The shell felt disgusting, my hand opened in repudiation, let it drop, took hold of Matthew's hand and clung.

"Come on, I'm ravenous," he said. "What's for lunch?"

Lightning and thunder split and rent the dark day-sky.

Rain drenched down. In the sudden alien gloom we finished lunch and watched the deluge.

The end of the long drought. The previous day, at the Prime Minister's request, churches throughout the country had prayed for rain.

A pause in the noisy downpour allowed thunder to rumble on while ghastly forks of lightning stabbed the earth.

"Aren't you afraid?" he asked.

"What you do to me! I've always been petrified of storms. Today I find it—exhilarating."

We got up, began to clear the table. A flash! An electric shock crackled through the cottage. I was in his arms, plates and all. My laughter was shaky.

Later the sun burst forth. Scarlet and purple clouds trumpeted its evening victory. We walked along the firm beach. When we left the shore to enter the belt of jungle, using the path which arrived eventually at the village with its few stores, a man strolled toward us, a Zulu in a black cowboy hat. He was strumming a yellow and brown guitar, melodious, monotonous. He passed us and went on toward the sea, the music growing fainter in the gathering dusk until there was only the sound of countless raindrops dripping from the dense foliage . . .

That night Matthew said, "The lagoon will have mucked up the sea, we won't be able to bathe tomorrow and . . . anyway, there's something I must do . . ."

Thus with studied carelessness he fractured the stillness of our days.

Next morning I collected a key from the local house agent . . . I insisted I should do it, that it would be wiser;

Matthew might, after all, be recognized on some future occasion . . . and I bought supplies from the general store, then together we went to an empty beach cottage, moved in the supplies for—as he put it in his throwaway manner—"someone who might have to go underground."

One more day, our last night. We cleared away the supper things, had a brisk walk—the night was chilly after the rains—and went to bed. We made love, there was a tension yet it was part of those idyllic days, a rounding off, a suitable conclusion. We said good night—a formal gesture —kissed, and lay quietly . . . I wondered how life could ever be "normal" again. Yet I knew we would, in the morning, make a competent, leisurely departure. The dull weight of misery and anticlimax would be partially alleviated by transition . . .

In the darkness beyond the immediate moment the terrifying uncertainty forced itself upon me, it was in my throat to cry, Matthew, save us! when his mouth covered mine, crushing my words, his body heaved over mine, ferociously he entered me, I shuddered when he moved inside me, my hands beat against him, his assaults could not come angrily enough to defy and ward off that terrible, terrible dark . . .

Long after our storm had exhausted its violence we lay unmoving . . . stay on me, heavy, *here*, keep me, stay forever inside me, like this, now . . . That we must pull apart, and start our lives all over again! In all the hatred, the unloving, the destruction and separation, why can we not stay together, to love?

Chapter 18

*A*S I UNROLLED THE MORNING PAPER FOUR DAYS AFTER our return from the coast, a headline stood out with devastating clarity: KOBIE VERSFELD CAPTURED.

A day of mourning, blank. A day interminable, somehow to be survived. Under the dulled sun.

I went in the evening to meet Matthew. The hotel lounge we'd agreed on was musty, the furniture drab. I waited at a table near the main door. I found myself staring at the table surface, marked by the slops of innumerable glasses. The place was hot. I felt cold. The ash tray was blue aluminum, dented and scratched. I wished that I smoked. I ordered a brandy. Dread had fixed in certainty. You're not coming. Matthew, you've been arrested. Shall I phone the house, ask Mary? The waiter put the brandy down. I no longer wanted it. But if you've gone underground? That's it! If you don't come, you've gone, you're safe! I mustn't panic. If only you would leave the country. Anything but jail! The waste. We've had no life together, not to speak of, yet. Jail. No. What's the time? Ten past, and you so punctual. No, I mustn't think. I won't think . . .

And suddenly I felt his hand on my shoulder, he was there, beside me . . . the pressure of his hand tightened. And finally I could look at him.

We moved to a table in a dim corner and sat, gripping each other's hands, not speaking for a long while. His eyes were bloodshot. His face looked creased . . . weariness pervasive. Versfeld too, in those pictures of the capture . . . "Funny," I babbled, "I've just realized—he looked like Lenin!"

Matthew considered, his hand gestured vaguely. "Never occurred to me. He does, actually . . . I mean did." Eventually: "Strange, Annie, as if someone has died. The disguise was so effective, he was like a new person who I had to get to know, and became deeply attached to, and now . . ." He shook his head with a confused sadness, and smiled, as if he'd diverted essential grief at the capture of his friend into this tangential bereavement.

"To think he was right here all the time," I said. I sipped some brandy. "And you?" I dared to ask.

"My dear, it's an abominable mess at the moment. I have to see what pieces can be picked up."

"Oh God, Matthew! Survival's what matters! What earthly use . . . Look," I was desperate, "I mean either you survive or . . ."

He put a finger firmly on my mouth.

"There's no question. But to stay. However hopeless it seems, and ugly . . . It's the only possible thing. Our acts do matter. You know that."

I had nothing to say.

227

"If they question you . . . Oh my dear, sometimes I wish I'd never . . ."

This time it was I who silenced him, answering, "My love, what you said, about acts, about staying here, I understand . . . I know."

His eyes, burning, weary, searched mine. "Yes," he said. Happiness filled his face. "Yes, I see. Thank you." He lifted my hands, one then the other, to kiss. "Well," he went on— he sounded almost gay for a moment—"I shan't use that beach place, there's nothing you know that can help them . . . Alan will keep an eye on you." He paused, then, "They searched the house and my chambers today. No. Nothing to find." He grinned reassurance. "Besides," his grin widened, "they raided the homes of some highly respectable citizens. They're in a triumphant mood, a good sign, they could slip up through arrogance!"

His eyes sought the depths of my spirit. "Annie, just know . . . I love you. What we have—oh my beloved, what you've given to me!—why, your love is in and all around me, a part of life itself. And Annie, don't despair . . . ever. I agree with the Jesuits, that is a great sin!"

He kissed me, and abruptly had gone.

No no! Stay! He was already moving through the foyer, through the swinging doors, walking along the street, had disappeared.

Kobie Versfeld was brought to court three days later. The corridors clattered with uniformed police. The handful of spectators entered the galleries of a court bristling with Special Branch. It's not only the eyes, I thought, it's the backs of their necks. Their mood, as Matthew had said, was triumphant. I put on a bored expression, pretended to chat with Helen Mills and Walt beside me, waved at Ben who was with Sven Björnstrand and an American, but my heart pumped as, covertly, I watched those men.

While we waited I counted them, obscenely milling around the dock, forty-nine I'd got to, when from the cells up the steps into the dock came a small, slight, bespectacled man, rosy-faced, with silver hair beginning to reappear against a receding crop of auburn. Gone were the moustache and beard with their reminder of Lenin.

He turned calmly, deliberately, to look at his children and friends in the "white" gallery, then, turning to the "non-white" gallery, he greeted—he needed no gesture—the people who were there. The bitter resentment I had sporadically harboured against him was utterly dispelled.

The formality, the committal to trial, took a few minutes, then down to the cells he went.

"Never saw such a cowardly bunch of bastards! Marshalled a ruddy battalion! Kobie must be laughing his head off." Ben was describing the events of the morning for the benefit of friends who had not been present in court. We were on the terrace celebrating Jacob's birthday. Jake magnanimously allowed his guests to play with his new boxer puppy. We adults had our drinks. Nor was it an entirely unconvincing picture of a good party—as Shula said, the last thing Kobie Versfeld would want was long faces and a feeling of defeat.

"But I must tell you what happened after," continued Ben. "You know I took along Björnstrand and this American editor who's touring the country? Well, Björnstrand was pretty gloomy; Kobie—he said—looked like a nice fellow, a dreadful waste, and what was the use? Anything anyone did, the Government would win out. Then this American journalist, at the top of his voice, said, 'Say, they've got Versfeld, but what I wanna know is, where are the real Kremlin boys?' "

Which kept us amused for quite a while . . .

It was dark, the stars appeared one at a time, then all at once . . . Matthew, under these same stars, at least that much I knew . . . We sat, our bodies at peace on the face of the earth . . . Shulamuth, Ben, Alan, and Jill; I felt their presence and I was one of them . . .

Alan spoke. "Kobie today . . . I've been thinking of something Keith Gibbon said: that in a way we are lucky to belong here, appalling though things are . . . because any South African who is worth anything is going through the fire, and out of that, something valuable will be compounded. That is true for Kobie. And"—Alan's hand closed over mine—"it is true for Matt . . ."

One of the kids put a kwela record on, a couple of them began to gyrate . . . The simple repetitious music eased heart and brain . . . Awareness stirred, vibrated—my senses that can watch the stars, listen to the crickets, smell the first petunias of the summer, can love such a man . . . The penny whistles began to wheedle, the rhythm and beat to pound. I began to respond, shoulders slightly hunched, elbows a bit bent, head gently jerking, till it couldn't be contained and I too gyrated, hips moving through to knees, up and down onto flattened feet, shifting ground delicately, deliberately, shoulders still, hips swivel, head forward, back, forward—"Hey! Anne's got it!" called Jake—shuffle now, a subtler beat, head shaking, matchstick legs arms lift contract, foot just so—flat, still—swivel on it forward back . . . Matthew, wherever you are, can you feel my feeling? My hunger . . . ?

Jake was saying good night to me. "D'you think Uncle Matt will come soon?" he asked. "To see my puppy?"

The first rooster crows. Dawn at last. "Douvoordag" . . . your voice . . . the imprint of your head was long ago shaken from my pillow, your seed laundered from the sheet . . . A dog barks. Silence. A car honks and an engine revs up. Is it them? Silence. I twist with the pain of severance . . . Matthew. Where? Safe? Awake? . . . Loud reports, all the dogs in the neighbourhood bark, but there are always shots in the night. A car engine, quite loud. My heart thuds, my windpipe constricts. If it's them they must surely smell the stink of fear. Will I disintegrate, spew out mean little meaningless facts? My eyes strain. Perhaps turn on you like a vicious mouse? Silence. Bones and organs melt inside my flesh. The gloomy honking of a train. Passport's in order, why not? . . . Leave? Leave you, leave this place? To go, actually to get into the airways bus and drive to the airport? Simply out of the question. How did you put it? "To stay is the only possible thing."

The recognition steadied me and I slept.

A persistent knocking wakened me. The sun was just

coming up. I slipped on my dressing gown and went to the veranda door. The small girl in the yellow dress was there and, beyond her in the shadows, a man. Nathaniel.

"Nathaniel! Quick, come inside." And when he was in, "Are you all right? Can I get you something?"

His face was like a black skull. He grinned, shook his head positively, and asked, "Mr. Marais, is he in the city?" I told him Matthew was away, I did not know where. "I must find him, I think I know the place," he said.

"I'll take you. Where is he?"

He told me, it was not far from the city. He suddenly sat down, utterly worn out, and, studying his face, I noticed it was swollen on one side, with a blue-gray sheen. I hurried to get him bread and cheese and coffee. "Eat something, do," I begged and, struck now by the impression of a man grimy, in dusty rumpled suit, a man on the run, "Look, there's the bathroom." He cocked his hand to his brow in a salute that was half mocking. While I threw on my clothes I heard the lavatory flush, the taps running, then silence. And all the while through anxiety, through fear, through my frantic haste, threaded the music of the thought that soon I would see Matthew.

When I returned to the living room Nathaniel was dozing in the chair. He'd hardly touched the food. The rustling of paper as I wrapped it to take on the journey aroused him. He must have been living on his nerves and without sleep for days.

"Hurry!" he urged, unnecessarily.

The map was in the car. Sunlight filtered coolly through the trees which hummed with the activity and early songs

of birds as we drove off. I made sure we were not followed.
It was not until we waited impatiently for a garage attendant to fill the gas tank that I paused to consider: how did
Nathaniel escape? Or, if he did not escape but was freed
after giving evidence, what was he doing here? I watched
him covertly—he'd begun hungrily to munch the bread
and cheese—and in me suspicion ballooned: he's become
an informer, he's using me to track down Matthew for
them.

I drove fast through almost empty streets toward the
northwest and began carefully to sound him out.

"I heard you'd been arrested."

He grunted, his mouth was full of food, then: "They
gave me hell. I tell you, man, it was hell!" He laughed with
grim defiance.

"How long were you in for?"

"Ach man, too long! I gave up counting."

Was he evading? Why had he said nothing about turning
State witness? Then I saw how unfair—it was hardly something one would announce—and I felt guilty, remorseful
that I'd not been more welcoming, had not marvelled that
he was free, besides, those bruises looked painful. And
yet . . .

"Fantastic that you're free," I said. "How on
earth . . . ?"

Spurred by my question, or by his own sense of release
now that we had emerged from the city and its suburbs and
were racing along the highway toward our destination, he
began spontaneously to talk.

"They broke me down, they got a statement out of me."

He looked bitterly at me, then nodded. "I can see you were told. So, they kept me locked up a long time after. Not in solitary, mind, oh no, those guys are pretty smart; no, they had me in with three others, I knew their game, they had us all watching each other, trying to trick each other and find out what was what. Two of those bastards—you will excuse my terminology—they were impimpis!" Again that tone of scathing contempt I'd heard resounding in my mind. "Ach, but that is past. You want to know how I am free?" And he began to laugh loudly, with a mad sort of joy. "They brought me to court, you see, to give evidence against a poor lazy devil of a friend of mine, and when I get into the box, what do I see but Mfaxa grinning at me like a fat cat and I thought, hell, this baby is going to wipe that grin off that silly fat face. 'Your Worship,' I say, 'I do not want to give evidence.' You should have seen that Mfaxa! That was a sight for the gods. Yes, man, that was a great moment in my life!"

He clapped his hands, and clapped one hand to his head, imitating Mfaxa's woe; I had to slow down as I watched and laughed and urged him to tell what happened next.

"Fast talking was needed or Mfaxa and his gang would get the Magistrate to shut me down so, fast, I said, 'I was forced to make a statement under torture, Your Worship, I made the statement when I was not in my right mind. After, I asked to see it. Sgt. Mfaxa said no, it is against the law. I said, charge me or set me free. Then they brought my father to try to influence me. He said I must do what my conscience told me. I said again charge me or let me go.' By this time Mfaxa had been jabbering to the lieutenant and he jabbered to the Prosecutor, so I thought, time to wrap up. 'Your Worship,' I said, 'it would be wrong for me to speak against a friend. I could not live with this. I know a man who gave evidence against his friends and he has become a drunkard . . .' and that was the last word I could say because the Prosecutor had been up and the Magistrate had been trying to shut me down and next thing he sentenced me to a year for refusing to give evidence!" At the thought of this and of his escape, Nathaniel let out a mocking cry.

I was so enthralled by the splendour of his courage I'd forgotten to watch the road signs. "What is this place we're going to?" I belatedly thought to ask.

"A house, sort of staging post." His face contorted, I recognized mistrust. "It is safe to tell you?" he asked.

I smiled at the nonsense of the question. He began to grin. "I'm glad you were suspicious too," I said, laughing with relief.

"I, impimpi! You thought that!" Outraged, he rounded on me. I felt that the black wrath, for so long held in check and which, even in his brief narrative, was characteristically vented through mockery, was about to explode. Then he, too, saw the humour of it and our quick hilarity became a celebration of his escape.

"A staging post for people who have to cross the border," he eventually explained. "I am on my way!"

"Marvellous! But you still haven't told how?"

I drew up and motioned to him to save his story until we'd studied the map. Behind us the sun blazed. The car sent a long shadow before us on the highway. The turn we wanted was only a few miles on. Again we sped forward. There was not much traffic.

"It was the prison van," he said. "We were locked in and driven from the court, there was an accident, we could not see how it happened but suddenly we crashed onto the side, the cage was broken . . ."

"Are you all right?" I interrupted anxiously.

"Man, after Mfaxa's tortures, a car crash is nothing!" He paused, and I wondered at his gift for understatement. "Well, there were four of us, we did not wait to see what happened to Mfaxa and the driver, we just ran and ran and ran, but I did not trust the others, I gave them the slip, they were running and running, they looked like scared rabbits, it was funny, so I stopped and hid and then went off on my own."

The spurt of vitality had drained from him. His head drooping against the seat; he just had time to ask for news of Beatrice and to listen to my report about the reduced sentence before he again dozed. He slept with such stillness that he might have stopped breathing; his face turned toward me was deathly tired and held a sort of lost innocence . . .

The route now lay along a narrow dirt road. Would it be better to wait until dark? Surely not . . . danger might come, rather, with delay.

At last we approached the dorp. I stopped and told Nathaniel to wake up, had to shake him, then he came wide awake but looked suddenly old. I said he should sit in the back, we were less likely to attract attention if he was the

gardener and I the madam. He did so and adjusted his posture to what he thought suitably subservient, giving us cause
for renewed laughter, but now our laughter held a harsh
note of tension. As we went on I watched for a local in-
habitant from whom we could ask the way. A barefoot old
man was walking toward us. I slowed down. Nathaniel
questioned him. Miraculously he knew the road we wanted.
Driving on, I felt this omen signified that Matthew would be
there ready to organize Nathaniel's safe journey to the
border. And when we are with Matthew, I told myself,
Nathaniel can hear about the plans we've made. Matthew
. . . if Versfeld's disguise was so convincing that he could
live freely, all those months, then Matthew, too . . .

We'd reached the road. Caution was vital. Another good
omen: trees grew along each side of the pavement. We
drove at normal speed past the houses—well-spaced bun-
galows—some with families or servants moving about in the
grounds. The number we sought must be at the far end.
There was little traffic, a car or two, Africans on bicycles.
The gardens were now more like allotments . . . and
ahead was an inconspicuous house, its hedges untrimmed.
This was it. No sign of life. Was Matthew inside? I had to
force myself not to brake, not to run immediately to the
front door, but to drive innocently past.

On the other side of the house two cars were parked. A
Volkswagen and a big American car.

"Don't stop!" Nathaniel ordered. "Go straight on, then
we can see."

At a reasonable distance, with trees and bushes for cover,
I parked and, beyond minding now whether the inhabitants

observed or not, I raced back, taking as much care as possible to keep out of view of the house itself, until, breathless, I stood among the dense shrubs that bordered the overgrown garden. Nathaniel was right behind me. We gazed fixedly at the side door of the house which was opening . . . a man came out. He was tall, quite young and sprucely dressed. Then another . . . I thought I'd seen the first man in the crowd milling round Versfeld in court . . . they both carried revolvers.

And suddenly beyond, in the passageway, unmistakably, Matthew's pale face, his angular form . . . Now he came out . . . he had the beginnings of a beard and he was handcuffed to a heavily built man who, to make doubly sure, held fast to his arm.

They all paused—someone had called from inside the house—the three S.B. turned toward the door. As they did so, Matthew looked around the garden; he must be instinctively considering the chances of making a break for it; I thrust forward, pushed aside a branch and, distant though we were, he and I were abruptly face to face.

He stared for a long moment in shock and wonder, then, very slightly but with deliberation, he shook his head. The man to whom he was handcuffed must have felt the tug and jabbed at his arm to remind him that the steel grip was inescapable. Our gaze was torn asunder.

Now the group was joined by another member of the S.B. and, following him like a cur coming to heel, was Jolobe.

Matthew was being hustled into the back of the big car, his guard beside him. The spruce man sat with the driver.

The car started up and reversed rapidly toward where we were crouched in the bushes. Matthew turned as though casually to look through the rear window . . . when he saw me his eyes blazed with an intensity of love and encouragement. The car swung away. Through the side window I had a last glimpse of him.

"There was nothing we could do," said Nathaniel, furious, desolate. "Nothing!"

The fourth man and Jolobe were going into the house again, no doubt to search.

Nathaniel took my arm to lead me to the car. I caught myself grinning the idiot grin that usurps one's mouth in the face of calamity . . .

"We must find a telephone," I said.

In the main street of the dorp we found a garage with a phone booth. I asked for Alan's number and waited . . . I was anxious for Nathaniel but he lay low in the car. At last, Alan's voice: "Anne . . . I can hardly hear you." And when, loudly, I'd explained—"Anne dear, come straight to my office. Meanwhile I'll get on to Pretoria . . . Yes, he's sure to be taken there. I'm afraid there's little chance they'll tell me more than that . . ." Confirming what I'd already dreaded: A hundred and eighty days, Pretoria prison, and no legal redress.

"It is one hell of a shame," said Nathaniel.

"What will you do? Shall I drive you to the border?"

"I appreciate that, Anne, I truly do, but I will take a train, less risky, more usual—there is one packed with migrant workers which crosses the border very late at night . . . the police get careless."

"I certainly hope so." Then I busied myself with a notebook and pencil and quickly wrote down addresses for him in London, explained about the scholarship, stuffed into his pocket all the money I had, and silenced his thanks.

There was nothing left to do but drive fast back to the city . . . Matthew, I calculated, must already have reached Pretoria. They would have taken the direct road . . . was he locked inside a cell? Or—Matthew . . . are they interrogating you, now? Forcing you to stand! Matthew, you, riding the breakers, free . . . And at last I wept. Had to stop the car as, with all defences down, grief raged through me . . .

Nathaniel did not utter a word. It seemed to me he did not stir, only was there, with me. Then in dull exhaustion I rested my face against the driving wheel.

It was not until I prepared to drive on that he spoke. "Beatrice and my father will share your sorrow."

"I hope she does not hear of it."

"We have learned to live with the truth. And you, what will you do? Perhaps return to England?"

"No. This is my home. My life is here."

We were approaching the city. I headed for the station, turned the last corner . . . in front of us two black women gossiped. I tooted. They leaped into the air and began to screech with laughter, then went on their way.

I parked at a discreet distance from the Non-Whites Only entrance.

Nathaniel was about to get out when he turned back to face me. "I was not going to tell you, but you also have learned to live with the truth. I will not take the scholarship. No, don't speak!" He grinned at the fierceness of his demand, but he was dead serious. "I want you to understand—besides, maybe one day you can tell my father and Beatrice; Matthew Marais, too. It's like this—when those devils drive you crazy with pain, you hate. Jesus, but you hate!" He broke off and watched me. "You know now, don't you, Anne, what it is to hate?"

My throat had tightened at his words, my hands were clenched. Yes, I knew now.

"I, too," he said, "I had not learned before what it is, truly, to hate. And I wanted to kill, blindly. That's bad, wasteful. Afterward, I saw everything straight and clear. That's good. I saw that there is no way forward except through violence, only it must be controlled, it must be very carefully and deliberately planned. Another thing, when I stood in that witness box and refused to talk, when I saw those faces—the Magistrate, the Prosecutor, Mfaxa —I felt free. I got a taste—I got greedy for freedom!" His quiet laughter became a confirmation of this liberation before, soberly, he went on. "I am going for guerrilla training. Our brains, our bodies, must be made one with our weapons. How else can we destroy these devils? How else can we, the black people, win back our land and our dignity?"

His bony hand held mine hard. Then casually, as though it were an everyday occurrence, this journey ahead of him, we said good-bye and he slipped from the car.

"Good luck!" I called after him. And, "Take care," I whispered as I watched him join the throng of black men and women who hurried for their trains. He might be very weary but he moved proudly and with the same sinewy assertiveness I remembered from our walk along the seashore. A confident wave of his hand and he moved out of sight.

I drove slowly through the thrusting noisy crowd which spilled from the pavements onto the street . . . Yes, I thought, my life is here. I shall visit Matthew when I can, to say nothing much through the barrier. I shall write him five-hundred-word letters, when I can. I shall write—how did Matthew once put it?—"bear witness," for as long as I can. And each day I shall awaken to familiar sunlight, to the familiar sound of doves . . .

AFTERWORD

South Africa in 1965: as Ben Lowen puts it in the novel, though the sabotage has been well and truly crushed, the Security Police continue "bulldozing every crumb of protest". He is referring to the Eastern Cape. Yet within a few years Steve Biko and other young Blacks from that area were to found the Black Consciousness Movement, helping to inspire the 1976 uprising when Black schoolchildren in Soweto confronted heavily armed police. When the shootings began, and Hector Pieterson was killed, they retaliated with their only weapons, sticks and stones — "The day our kids grew up" The Sowetan newspaper was to call it. As the infuriated protest spread hundreds more were shot dead while others fled the country to give a new impetus to the ANC's sabotage movement which in time turned to guerrilla activity and sporadic bombings.

By 1985, the country was racked by racial unrest which had been stimulated by President Botha's cruelly inadequate reforms. On 21 March, the twenty-fifth anniversary of the Sharpeville massacre, police in the Eastern Cape fired on a crowd of unarmed Blacks going to the funeral of a student killed by police; twenty-nine men, women and youths were shot dead. Riots swept the land. And the outside world — as never before — became aware of the savage violence of the state: day after day, television news revealed police and army, Black as well as white, invading townships and from their armoured vehicles shooting people — children too — as though they were big game, and *sjambokking* protestors, white as well as Black. Following the detention of

243

community leaders, churchmen, trade unionists and students, enraged crowds fought "the system", stoning and petrol-bombing police and collaborators — suspects as well. The government clamped down with successively more devastating states of emergency, giving police immunity from prosecution and imposing harsh censorship. It treated with contempt the calls from international as well as local leaders for negotiation with the outlawed ANC and for the release of Nelson Mandela and the other political prisoners — among them Govan Mbeki on whom the character of Daniel Makhana was based. Mbeki, now in his late seventies, was released, after twenty-four years on Robben Island only to be placed under stringent restrictions and confined to Port Elizabeth.

Matthew Marais's remark in the novel, that the vital task is to expose what is going on in the Eastern Cape, has acquired a terrible resonance through the decades as the actual Lubbes and Mfaxas have killed or attempted to break innumerable men, women and children. Various tortures endured by one young woman they detained during 1976, culminated in a wet towel being placed over her head, then repeatedly pulled tight until she was almost suffocated, almost strangled. When eventually the towel was loosened, she was asked, "Now can you see how Mohapi died?" Mapetla Mohapi had been hanged in his cell, an alleged suicide. Soon after, when Steve Biko, a close friend of Mohapi's, was detained, in the cell he found a doll hanging by its neck with a note which read: "Mapetla welcomes you."

A year later, while again in detention, Biko himself was slowly and horribly done to death. The Security Police of the Eastern Cape had achieved world-wide notoriety. But were undeterred. In September 1985 three detainees from Biko's home village, Ginsberg, died within hours of their arrest. One was only fifteen years old.

In Port Elizabeth it seemed there might be momentary relief

when a brave district surgeon, Dr Wendy Orr, produced over-whelming evidence that detainess were being "systematically assaulted and abused". She had defied the instructions of her superior, Dr Ivor Lang, the very man belatedly censured by South Africa's Medical and Dental Council for disgraceful conduct in the handling of the Biko case. She was promptly transferred to a job visiting old people's homes. However, a judge did grant an order restraining police from assaulting prisoners in two local jails; one of them was North End, alias Rooihell.

Torture and deaths in detention have of course occurred throughout the country, but in 1985 when Cape Town University's Institute of Criminology found that 93 per cent of thousands of Black detainees suffered some form of physical abuse, they reported a higher incidence in the Eastern Cape. Between 1986 and 1987 some 25,000 detainees were held, more than 10,000 of them under the age of eighteen. Children have been beaten with rifle butts, half-suffocated with wet nylon bags and subjected to electric shock torture.

A horrifying element through the years has been the role of *impimpis* — informers. Their betrayals, their concocted evidence, have caused excruciating suffering and not surprisingly it was in the Eastern Cape that revenge by the gruesome "necklace" first occurred — a rubber tyre filled with petrol was placed around the suspect's neck and set alight. As killings by police multiplied — a thousand, two thousand deaths — crowd ferocity intensified and on occasion the victim was forced to light the match which fired the petrol. Who could tell how rumour and accusations of collaboration or informing, were started? As far back as 1962 when a wave of intimidation and terror swept New Brighton township, police — adept *agents provocateurs* — were observed disguised as *tsotsis* and loafers; by 1987 they were seen instigating vigilante rampages in which Black trade unionists, young comrades and other protesters have been killed or injured. State propaganda calls this Black on Black violence.

Against this background Port Elizabeth's 350,000 Black residents, tired of waiting for the troops to withdraw from the townships and for their community leaders to be released from detention, mounted a boycott of white-owned shops which for a while was spectacularly successful. But desperate white business-men who begged the government for reforms were rebuffed; the boycott organizers were detained. New Brighton and Kwazakhele townships were surrounded by high razor-wire entanglements with exit and entrance guarded by security forces. Meanwhile Port Elizabeth faced ruin; Black unemployment soared.

Despite this massive repression, despite the continuing bull-dozing and forced removal of rebellious neighbourhoods, the countrywide United Democratic Front, Black trades unions and a recently formed national Youth Congress continue to function, organizing strikes, with many organizers somehow surviving underground. Today it is unthinkable that young Blacks could be humiliated as was the youth induced to admit he was "dead happy" with his lot under apartheid. Boldly, recklessly they now taunt the police, risking death. Their parents, too, risk imprison-ment and eviction as they join in the rent boycott which has become a vital form of protest. And whereas in 1965 no one would have dared to speak of the African National Congress — they might have referred to it as the "big thing" — today it is openly talked of as if it were a football team.

But I want to tell about recent happenings in the dorp in which I placed the Qaba family. Incidentally there was no Beatrice Qaba, just as there was no Nathaniel, although her character was partly based on an extraordinarily courageous nursing sister from Port Elizabeth who continued to be persecuted long after serving her sentence. The dorp was Cradock. And Anne Dawson's encounter with Samuel Qaba was based on two visits I paid to

Canon James Calata in 1961 and 1965. Calata was quite different to Qaba: thin, with a strongly-lined face and a rich voice, he had been Secretary-General of the ANC from the thirties until 1949 when he was replaced by Walter Sisulu. It was he, almost single-handedly and despite illness and poverty, who had revived the organization at a time of its most serious decline. A musician, he composed stirring freedom songs for the ANC. I had met him in Johannesburg during 1957 when he was among the 156 defendants in the Treason Trial. In the sixties my first visit took place shortly after he had again been on trial, this time for having on his walls two photographs — one taken in 1939 of him as President of the Cape ANC, the other of a 1942 Congress delegation to the Deputy Prime Minister. Imprisoned for twelve days before being brought to trial, he was then found guilty of "displaying" pictures of an "unlawful organisation"; sentenced to six months he was awaiting the result of an appeal. The appeal was to fail; the sentence was confirmed, but suspended. Calata wrote to me:

The picture case was not too great a disappointment except the criminal stain in the face of the public. I did not expect the judge to stoop down to politics. I feel no breach of my conscience over those pictures. It is one of those persecution measures which I have become used to and am leaving it to God who can turn it to some good.

Revisiting Cradock in 1965, I found that the "location" of which his mission had been a part, had been eradicated. Two miles away in an arid landscape was the new "township", called Lingelihle. As he was banned and under partial house arrest we did not attempt to meet there, but had tea with one of his white friends in Cradock. He was now seventy but upright as ever.

He died at the age of eighty-eight and was given a hero's funeral. By 1983 funerals had become the opportunity for political protest and his coffin was draped in the illegal ANC black, green and gold flag. The youths who carried his coffin sang the illegal freedom songs he had composed. The procession accompanying his body to the grave was followed by Security Police.

Within two years Cradock was described as the "hottest spot in the backveld revolution" sweeping the country. Led by Lingelihle's immensely popular acting headmaster, Matthew Goniwe, son of a domestic servant and a seller of firewood, a Residents' Association was demanding urgent reforms in the dusty, poverty-stricken place. Working with the youth — most of them with no hope of jobs — Goniwe raised educational standards and gave them self-respect, stopping much of their drinking and dagga smoking. CRADORA organized funerals, street cleaning, the maintenance of order and help for bereaved families. Goniwe's dismissal and repeated arrest only hardened the people's resistance. Accused of "agitating", he remarked, "Agitation is not required when you have apartheid — the greatest agitator of all." His close associate was Canon Calata's grandson, Fort, so named because he had been born at the time of the Treason Trial when his grandfather was imprisoned in the Johannesburg Fort.

In June 1985 these two young men with Sparrow Mkonto and an activist from a neighbouring village, were driving back to Cradock from a meeting in Port Elizabeth when they disappeared. Days later their bodies were discovered — all had been repeatedly stabbed then, after death, burned. 50,000 people from all over South Africa attended their funeral, a sombre and disciplined display of opposition to the government but also a celebration of their lives. At the graveside stood their four widows. One of the speakers was Victoria Mxenge, who had also spoken at Canon Calata's funeral. Two weeks later she herself was assassinated, just as her husband, Griffiths, had been, four years earlier.

The Mxenges were among the younger lawyers of all races now active in innumerable political trials.

I can imagine Matthew Marais and Anne Dawson driving in a packed Combi from Johannesburg to Cradock to attend the funeral of Goniwe and his friends. They might well have known the young men, and Anne could have kept up her connection with people in Cradock. If so, she would have met Molly Blackburn, to whom Goniwe turned for advice in the technicalities of setting up CRADORA. Molly was one of a new generation of whites in the Eastern Cape, prepared to work with and identify with these young Black leaders, a very different role to the kind, tweedy woman who took food to Beatrice Qaba. But soon Molly too was dead, killed in a car crash. Again I can see Matthew and Anne at the extraordinary funeral in Port Elizabeth when thousands of Blacks poured into the heart of the city to mourn her, while armed police and frightened whites watched.

To go back to the sixties and what might have happened to Matthew and Anne after his imprisonment — at least five years for assisting men to leave the country. In Pretoria prison Kobie Versfeld was in a nearby cell. By day, from a courtyard where they grew flowers and fruit trees, they could glimpse the sky, but their small cell windows could not capture its magnificence at night.

Released from prison, Matthew would have been placed under partial house arrest, restricted to Johannesburg and banned — but worse, he would have been disbarred. The bans prevented the sort of alternative activity he might have turned to such as working with trades unions, in education or for a newspaper. Nor could he visit any Black areas. He could meet with only one person at a time. Anne, meanwhile, was writing for both local and American newspapers — one of an increasing number of women among the outstanding journalists challenging Draconian censorship. I see her married to Matthew and, as he continued discreetly to play a role in the struggle, she would act as a go-between.

Paula, on her release, would emigrate to Israel. Soon she would be among the outspoken few, criticizing West Bank settlement and the activities of the security services.

And Anne's cousins would join the exodus to Australia — in any event she and they had long before broken off their uneasy relationship.

By the 1980s most of the bannings had been allowed to lapse. To celebrate his sudden freedom, Matthew and Anne leave the thrusting city with its vast spread, upward and outward, its buildings and homes and shopping malls all heavily guarded. Driving along super-highways they head for the cottage by the sea. This small refuge at least is unchanged. Beyond the sands, on the edge of the Indian Ocean, there are still rock pools to crouch over; I see the two of them — both now in their fifties — gazing by the hour into the miniature underwater worlds.

Never far from thought, a "living presence" as Matthew Marais called them, are those who have sacrificed themselves — those serving terms of life imprisonment, among them Mandela and Sisulu; those killed, among them Biko and Goniwe, twelve-year-old Hector Pieterson and the untold numbers of children, and Ruth First, assassinated in exile; and those who have died in prison, among them "Jakob Versfeld" who of course was a barely disguised Bram Fischer. We South Africans have a heritage of love from them, they enliven us.

Mary Benson, London, December 1987